Coltaine's Revenge

After six months of searching, Lewis Coltaine tracked down Emerson Greeley, the man who had murdered his wife. Lewis was hell-bent on vengeance but before Emerson died, he taunted Lewis with the promise that even after his death he'd find no peace. Lewis dismissed the taunt, but when he returned to his family home, Emerson's chilling threat had already come to pass. Lewis's eldest brother had been murdered.

Lewis's surviving brothers now vow to find the man responsible for destroying their family, but the clues point to the murder being connected to a dark, long-buried family secret. With the revelations he uncovers threatening to tear the family apart, can Lewis Coltaine finally deliver his revenge?

Coltaine's Revenge

Scott Connor

A Black Horse Western

ROBERT HALE · LONDON

© Scott Connor 2010
First published in Great Britain 2010

ISBN 978-0-7090-8987-2

Robert Hale Limited
Clerkenwell House
Clerkenwell Green
London EC1R 0HT

www.halebooks.com

Typeset by
Derek Doyle & Associates, Shaw Heath
Printed and bound in Great Britain by
CPI Antony Rowe, Chippenham and Eastbourne

CHAPTER 1

Three men stood on the wooden platform at Randall's End, watching the approaching train.

They remained motionless while the engine trundled past them, screeching as it slowed to a halt. A series of silent messages passed between them – a raised eyebrow from one man, a slow nod from another – which led to two of the men spreading out.

The third man, Greg Chester, stepped backwards to survey the scene. From under a lowered brim he watched the train halt, running his gaze across the three cars. Few people were inside and none of them was moving to leave.

Five minutes passed before a man stood and made his way down the aisle, walking bent over as if he were hiding. His progress was slow until he reached the door where he stopped and straightened, his form presenting an indistinct shadow on the grimy windowpane.

He waited as the train took on water, his reluctance

in leaving encouraging the two men closest to the train to look back at Greg for instructions. Greg gave them a nod, so they resumed their careful watching of the man.

Several more minutes passed until the engineer leaned out of the engine to shout that the train was ready to move out. A loud peel from the bell sounded before the train lurched into motion.

Only then did the man throw open the door, letting Greg see that he was short, plump, and had no baggage. He was not at all what Greg had expected to meet so when he jumped down on to the platform, he glanced at the other doors, but nobody else was making a late move to leave.

'You the only man getting off?' Greg called out.

The man looked at the train, now edging away from the platform, then shuffled round to face him.

'Just me,' he murmured, his eyes downcast, his tone uncertain as he rocked from foot to foot. His motion let Greg see that he wasn't packing a gun – also contravening everything he'd expected. 'Are you Greg Chester?'

'Yup. And who are you?'

The man gulped before he replied, his voice now shaking.

'I'm Lewis Coltaine. So now that I'm here, tell me what you want.'

This confirmation of his name made the two men standing before Greg settle their stances. Greg's only visible response was to raise an eyebrow.

6

'Not here,' he said. 'You're coming with us.'

'Not until you tell me whether you work for Emerson Greeley or Maxwell Templeton.'

It was the former, but Greg reckoned he didn't need to reveal that, especially as he'd made a decision.

'You're not Lewis Coltaine,' he said.

'Why do you say that?'

'Because you're fat, scared and unarmed.'

'I . . . I. . . .' The man waved his arms as he struggled to find an answer, but then his eyes darted to the side, the motion providing Greg with all the answers he needed.

He turned and saw movement behind the departing train. A man had jumped down from the last car and was walking down the tracks towards them. This man was everything the other man wasn't: rangy, confident and armed.

Greg went for his gun a moment before a blast of light exploded from the newcomer's gun. Hot fire punched him in the chest, sending him reeling backwards to land on the platform.

Two more crisp shots rang out followed by the thud of bodies hitting the wood.

Greg tried to rise, but his limbs ignored him and he could do nothing but lie on his back looking at the sky. All his fading energy went into making his punctured chest rise and fall to drag in each tortured breath.

'You got 'em,' said the man who had claimed to be

Lewis Coltaine.

'Thanks to you,' the other man said, his footfalls clumping as he joined him on the platform. 'Now, who are they?'

'I don't know, Lewis. I did what you asked, but they wouldn't tell me whether Emerson Greeley or Maxwell Templeton sent them.'

The newcomer, Lewis, snorted. Then footfalls echoed as he paced around the shot men. Contented grunts suggested both men were dead. Then his footfalls approached him and let Greg see the face of the man he'd come for.

They exchanged eye contact. Lewis's gaze was piercing; Greg's was watering. Then Lewis smiled.

'As you've still got some life left in you,' he said, 'you'll oblige me with a name.'

'How long will he be?' Cameron Coltaine asked, peering into the dark.

'Don't know,' his younger brother Harlan said, 'but Jesse's eyes aren't what they used to be. Perhaps he got lost in the dark.'

Cameron nodded. 'And to the ridge and back is a long way to walk, so perhaps his tired old legs have cramped up.'

Harlan laughed. Jesse was only forty, but he was the eldest of the Coltaine brothers and jokes about his age had always amused his brothers.

'Perhaps we should investigate,' Harlan said, his voice still light and joking.

Cameron could see the worry in his younger brother's eyes, but he also welcomed the way he was trying to make light of the situation. Not that there should be anything to worry about.

Two hours before Jesse had told Cameron's wife that he was going up the ridge that overlooked the small farm in which the three brothers lived. At sundown Harlan had seen him silhouetted against the skyline, but they hadn't seen him since.

With the darkness now spreading, they had to accept that even someone who had lived all his life traipsing around the gullies and crags along the ridge could have lost his footing in the poor light.

Cameron agreed they should go, so after shouting inside to their wives Mary and Esther, they left the house and, on foot, headed up the ridge. The rising moon was skidding behind low cloud at least giving them some light when they reached the point where Harlan had last seen Jesse.

Here a chill wind whipped dust around their legs, its steady rustling being the only sound they could hear. They could see the gully beyond the ridge now shrouded in deep shadows and appearing as an inky black hole.

There was still no sign of him.

Talking loudly so that Jesse would be able to hear them if he were close or in trouble, they debated their next actions. They agreed to separate, with Cameron making his way down into the gully and Harlan heading further along the ridge.

Again they murmured quick joking assurances to each other, but this time the comments didn't succeed in lightening either man's mood.

Then Cameron made his way down into the darkness, walking slowly to let his eyes become accustomed to the low light level. Above and to his side he could see Harlan pacing along, his form just a dark outline, until he too disappeared from view.

Cameron's night vision was letting him see more of the gully ahead when a gunshot blasted, the sound echoing. He froze, straining his hearing, and he heard a grunt of pain followed by a body hitting the ground then rolling. The noise had come from the position where he'd last seen Harlan.

Cameron scampered back up to the ridge. Despite not being armed, he gave no thought to his own safety as he hurried along the top.

Previously he had been worried only about the possibility that Jesse might have fallen into the gully, not that he might have encountered a problem that was more human in nature. Even now he hoped the gunshot had been a mistake or a way for someone to get his attention.

Even so, as he neared the point where he'd last seen Harlan, he ducked to limit his profile against the darkening sky.

He darted his gaze along the ridge then into the gully. On a ledge around thirty yards down there was an indistinct lighter form. Harlan's clothes were dark but Jesse had been wearing a light shirt and in the

10

gloom he thought with a rapidly sinking feeling that it could be his body.

Cameron paced down towards the form, hoping that he'd been mistaken but also looking around for whoever had fired if he hadn't.

When he jumped down to reach the ledge, he accepted he hadn't been mistaken: it was Jesse's body, lying still and unmoving.

As the shock overcame him, Cameron closed his eyes for a moment, then took a deep breath and rolled the body over.

Jesse sprawled on to his back to reveal a darkened patch on his shirt. Cameron dropped to his knees and felt his neck, then recoiled when Jesse dragged in a tortured breath. Then he spoke, the sound weak and gurgling.

'I couldn't hear that,' Cameron urged.

'Mason, Mason Crockett,' Jesse murmured.

The name meant nothing to Cameron and he urged Jesse to be calm, but Jesse uttered a rattling screech then arched his back before he flopped down and lay still.

Cameron leaned over him again and this time he couldn't feel a pulse. In shock, he looked up to the ridge to see the form of his younger brother peering down at the ledge, as he himself had done a few minutes earlier.

'Get down!' Cameron shouted.

'Are you all right?' Harlan asked, ducking slightly.

'I am, but Jesse isn't. He's ... he's dead, so get

right down. There's someone out there.'

'Who? Where?' Harlan demanded. This time he dropped out of sight.

Jesse's final words might have answered the first question but as Cameron peered into the darkness he was more worried about the second. He stayed on his knees and kept his profile as small and as low as possible while he waited for whoever was out there to come for him.

CHAPTER 2

On the outskirts of Liberty, Lewis Coltaine drew the horse he'd taken from Greg Chester to a halt.

He considered the small, deserted town, judging that all was as it seemed and that this time there would be no surprises, but he still dismounted and led his horse on a circuitous route to the stables. When he reached the door he was pleased he had been cautious, as from his new position he was able to see the horses outside the saloon. The one at the end was a pinto, a distinctive horse he recognized.

'So today Emerson Greeley nearly gets me,' Lewis said to himself, 'but it'll be me who gets him.'

Lewis was all too familiar with Emerson's ruses, so he wasn't excited about the possibility of ending his six month quest. After leaving his horse, he walked along beside the small corral at the side of the stables, taking a route that kept him out of sight from the saloon's front door and only window.

When he reached the end of the corral, he leaned

against the corner post.

If anyone were to see him they'd presume he was idling away his day or waiting for someone. But to avoid appearing as if that someone was in the saloon, he faced side-on to the building and only observed it from the corner of his eye.

As was his wont when he had time to spare, he withdrew his current journal from his pocket and recorded the morning's events, the act helping him to put his thoughts in order.

Two weeks before Lewis had been closing in on Emerson when he'd received a message from a man he'd never heard of called Greg Chester, saying he should go to Randall's End.

Over the last six months Lewis had paid many people to keep a lookout for Emerson. He had faithfully recorded their details in his journals and so he knew that Greg wasn't one of those people. When he'd also learnt that Randall's End was a rarely used station at which the train only ever stopped to take on water, he'd taken precautions against the possibility of it being a trap.

It had been, but before he'd died from his injury Greg had claimed that despite the ruse, Emerson Greeley had, in fact, holed up in the nearby town of Liberty.

So far it would appear that that this information was correct, even if as yet he hadn't seen Emerson, or for that matter anyone other than a young woman, who was walking towards him. Lewis kept writing while watching her from the corner of his eye.

'I know of you,' she said, coming to a halt. 'You're Lewis Coltaine and you're looking for Emerson Greeley.'

Lewis wrote down the last detail of the information that had led him here, then tucked the journal back into his pocket and looked up.

He nodded. 'You know Greg Chester?'

'Sure.'

'You keep bad company.'

She curled her lip in a sneer. 'Greg isn't important. All that matters is you're here. I want to hire you.'

Lewis flicked a casual glance at the saloon to confirm nothing was happening there.

'I'm not for hire. I'm on a—'

'I know. You're on a manhunt. I mean after you've dealt with Emerson.'

Lewis hadn't considered what he would do after he'd found Emerson. For the last six months that task had occupied his every waking moment, but even if his plans after that were non-existent, he knew one thing for sure.

'I'm still not for hire.'

'But it's a task you're suited to. I'm Elizabeth Fisher and I want you to kill the man who shot my husband.' She waited but when he didn't reply, she glanced out of town. 'I've been to Randall's End. I saw what happened there. I know you can do it.'

'Perhaps I can, Elizabeth Fisher,' Lewis said,

lowering his tone to an irritated growl. 'But like I said, I am not for hire.'

His change in tone made her stop trying to engage him in conversation then back away for a pace. But before she turned away, she gave him a beaming smile that said she had decided to leave of her own volition and that that had been just her opening attempt to hire him.

Lewis watched her walk away to ensure that she hadn't been trying to distract him for a more sinister reason. When she carried on past the saloon and disappeared into town, he dismissed her from his mind and concentrated on keeping an apparently disinterested eye on the saloon.

From then on nobody else approached him or even came into sight, letting Lewis prepare himself for what was about to happen.

He'd been waiting for an hour when the batwings creaked. A man emerged. He didn't look Lewis's way as he walked off down the boardwalk away from him.

Lewis's only sighting of Emerson six months earlier had been brief, but he was sure it was him, an observation that became more certain when the man headed to the pinto.

Originally Lewis had vowed to kill him on sight, but after what had happened to Raymond Templeton he was more cautious. He drew his gun and swung away from the corner post, then paced towards him. He didn't speak until he stepped up onto the boardwalk.

'Emerson Greeley,' he said, his voice loud enough to bring the man to a halt and remove the last lingering doubt from his mind that he had got the wrong man.

'So,' Emerson said, still looking away from him, 'Lewis Coltaine has found me at last.'

A short statement that he'd considered making many times over the last six months came to mind, but he didn't need Emerson to hear it. He just wanted to see his face for one last time so that Emerson could look into the eyes of his killer.

'I sure have. Raise those hands and turn around.'

'You'll regret following me.' Emerson moved his right hand away from his holster, but he still kept his back to him. 'You've walked into a trap.'

'I know, but I walked out of Randall's End alive.'

'You didn't think I put all my faith in Greg Chester, do you?' Emerson nodded towards the buildings across the road. 'I've got a man on the top of the mercantile, another in the saloon, and another behind you.'

Lewis was minded not to believe him, but the boardwalk on which he was standing wasn't covered and watchers could easily be hiding somewhere.

'You're lying, Emerson, and today I free my life from those lies.'

'You're wrong on both counts. I didn't lie, and if you do somehow manage to kill me, you won't get to enjoy your apparent victory.'

Slowly Emerson swung round to face him,

17

revealing an unconcerned expression despite the gun trained on his chest.

Lewis considered his composure, something he hadn't expected him to show, then flicked his gaze to the side to take in the opposite side of the road. He saw no sign of anyone.

Lewis moved his gun to sight Emerson's heart, minded to ignore whatever distraction he was trying to make, but when Emerson smiled, he decided to ask the question he obviously wanted him to ask.

'Why shouldn't I get peace after I've killed you?'

'Because in all your months of searching for me, you didn't uncover the most crucial fact.' Emerson raised his eyebrows. 'I didn't kill her.'

'More lies!'

'I did pull the trigger, but I didn't do it because I wanted to.' Emerson lowered his voice. 'I was hired.'

This was news to Lewis. He had never once considered that the version of events he'd accepted as being true might be wrong. He shook his head, his gaze again drifting to the mercantile roof, but at that moment Emerson jerked to the side and threw his hand to his gun.

His attempted distraction didn't work. Even with his gaze set elsewhere, Lewis fired. His slug tore into Emerson's chest and sent him reeling. Emerson's useless return shot wasted itself in the air.

Emerson landed on his side, then skidded across the boardwalk until he came to a crumpled halt. Lewis kept his gaze set on him as he paced past the saloon, sure now that there was no trap. He stopped before Emerson, his gun trained down at his forehead.

'Emerson Xavier Greeley,' he said, now deciding to deliver the words he'd considered saying when he had Emerson at his mercy. 'You murdered my wife and made me into a killer. You got any last words to say about that before you die?'

Emerson looked up at him through pained eyes that were glazing fast.

'Believe me,' he grunted between agony-filled gasps. 'I was hired and if you kill me, you'll never find the man who was really responsible . . . until it's too late and he sends you to hell.'

'I've been there. Today you take my place.'

Lewis moved forward, planning to drag more details out of him, but he heard the batwings creak behind him. He settled his stance then pulled the trigger.

Then he stood there, watching Emerson slump, twitch, be still until the only movement came from the steadily expanding pool of blood around his body. When it had stopped spreading, he holstered his gun and turned away.

He flinched, then stomped to a halt. Two guns were aimed at him, one from down the boardwalk, the other from the saloon doorway.

'Reach,' the man on the boardwalk said.

Lewis jerked his hands up to shoulder level.

'So Emerson spoke the truth, after all.'

'Emerson lied,' the man in the doorway said, then snorted a laugh. 'There is no man up on the mercantile roof. There's just us two.'

Lewis shrugged. 'Either way, you stepped in too late. Emerson's dead.'

'We don't care about him.' The man offered a cold smile, then beckoned Lewis to head to the stables. 'Maxwell Templeton sent us.'

'Why would anyone kill him?' Harlan Coltaine murmured.

'I don't know,' Cameron said, shrugging.

In the three hours that had passed since he'd found the body of his eldest brother, Cameron had asked himself that question many times and Marshal Ingersoll's questioning hadn't helped to bring him any answers.

They were now back in the house, with their wives and children safe and accounted for in one room. Jesse's body lay in the barn, the only place they could think of to put him, while Marshal Ingersoll and his two deputies scouted round.

'But whatever the reason, we can't leave this up to Ingersoll. We've got to act.'

Cameron saw the burning desire in Harlan's eyes to ride off and find the culprit – something he guessed others had seen in his own eyes – but Harlan was the one who might do it.

'And do what? We don't know who did this and—'

'We have a name. Jesse's last words were Mason

20

Crockett.'

'Yet we've never heard of him and we don't even know for sure that his last words meant that he was his killer.' Cameron raised a hand as Harlan started to object. 'We will act, but only when we know more, and only when we're sure our families are safe.'

The mention of family made Harlan utter a long sigh followed by a reluctant nod. Harlan had three children and Cameron two. Jesse didn't have a family of his own but with the three brothers sharing a sprawling house they had been as close as any family could be.

Harlan jutted his jaw and, because it was the unspoken thought on his own mind, Cameron knew what he was going to say before he said it.

'I know one thing we can do straight away,' Harlan said. 'We can visit the Miller brothers before they have time to gather up their addled wits.'

Cameron tipped back his hat while he pondered, but before he could decide whether this was something he wanted to do tonight, the door swung open to reveal the returned Marshal Ingersoll.

'I doubt any of them did it,' Ingersoll said.

'Why?' Cameron asked.

'For a start Thomas was getting some late lessons down at the school.'

'When I said the Miller brothers,' Harlan said, 'I didn't mean him.'

Every family had their black sheep: in the good hearted Coltaine family it was the argumentative

Lewis; in the good-for-nothing Miller family it was the studious Thomas.

'But it's the same with the other two. Jacob has been littering up a cell for the last week after he sold that rancid horse meat. Since I kicked him out, nobody's seen him leave their trading post.' Ingersoll raised a hand as both Cameron and Harlan started to say that this didn't mean he couldn't have done it. 'And Ward was in the saloon for most of the day. He'd be too drunk to have done this.'

'Or just drunk enough to do it,' Cameron said.

Ingersoll conceded this point with a rueful grunt.

'Perhaps, but I don't reckon they'd finally get themselves the courage to act after all these years.'

'But if it wasn't them, who else could it be? None of us have heard of Mason Crockett, and aside from the Miller brothers Jesse didn't have any enemies.'

Ingersoll shrugged. 'Those of us with long memories can remember another person who didn't like Jesse.'

'You mean Lewis?' Cameron asked, receiving a nod from Ingersoll. 'You're right that he and Jesse were always arguing, but Lewis didn't hate him enough to return and kill his own brother after all these years.'

Ingersoll shrugged and the three men stood in silence for a while until Ingersoll moved to leave, but before he slipped through the door he turned back.

'Whoever was responsible, you two will not confront the Miller brothers or anyone else you suspect. Once is enough in one lifetime. Understood?' He pointed a firm finger at each man until he received a nod. 'So if you come across any information or have any suspicions, you'll bring it to me and I'll deal with it.'

Ingersoll then headed outside, leaving the two men to stand in aggrieved silence.

'We accepting that?' Harlan said when they'd heard Ingersoll ride off.

'For now,' Cameron said. 'We'll wait until Jesse's in the ground and we've paid our respects. Then whether it's down to Mason Crockett, the Miller brothers, or even Lewis, we will make someone pay.'

CHAPTER 3

'When's Maxwell Templeton coming?' Lewis Coltaine asked, finally letting boredom goad him into speaking.

The sole man left guarding him, Wayne, sat back in his chair, the only other piece of furniture in the small building other than the chair Lewis was sitting on.

'Patience,' he snapped, his sharp tone showing he wasn't taking his own advice. 'He'll be here soon enough.'

The two men who had confronted Lewis in Liberty had escorted him at gunpoint to his horse then out of town. He hadn't been surprised to discover their destination was the station at Randall's End, although the sight that had greeted them there had shocked his companions out of their reasonable moods.

They'd frisked him, shoved him inside, tied him to a chair, then frisked him again for good measure before heading outside to discuss what they should do.

They'd agreed to take the bodies round to the back, then the younger one, Snyder, had left to fetch Maxwell.

That had been five hours ago. Now with the sun having set, Wayne was becoming agitated while Lewis sat idly in his chair and waited, watching the small area of land and sky that was visible to him through the open door.

Every few minutes Wayne jumped to his feet and pensively paced to the door to look outside, but he kept one eye on Lewis, not letting his placid demeanour lull him into a false sense of security.

The delay gave Lewis time to think.

Before he'd died, Emerson Greeley had claimed that someone had hired him and if that were true it invalidated everything that he had worked towards achieving. But his wife had had no enemies and nobody would have been minded to hire someone to kill her, so Lewis reckoned it was more likely that Emerson had spun a lie to distract him.

Maybe later, if he survived what was about to come, he would brood on whether there was any truth in his claim, but for now he dismissed it and steeled himself for an uncomfortable meeting.

Full darkness had descended when Wayne breathed a sigh of relief. Hoofbeats clopped a few moments later.

Snyder was the first to walk in with his face set in a

deep frown. He cast a significant glance at Wayne and shook his head.

This silent message made Wayne grunt, his tone low and sad, or perhaps even disgusted. When Maxwell Templeton walked in, Lewis understood the reason for their attitude.

He had met Maxwell only once before, shortly after Raymond's death, when he'd made an unsuccessful attempt to explain away what had happened. Then, Maxwell had been a fit and vital man. Since then, he'd gathered from a man Maxwell had sent after him that he wasn't well.

The husk of a man who stood in the doorway was in a worse state than Lewis had expected to see.

Maxwell was broadly the same age as Lewis's thirty-five years, but he was so stooped that, at first, he only looked at the floor before slowly his gaze rose to look at him. Rheumy eyes considered him before he shuffled inside. Even that motion made him dizzy and he staggered backwards into the wall.

He steadied himself and held out a hand. Getting his meaning, Snyder took his arm and escorted him to the other chair.

Maxwell flopped down into it and drew gasping wheezes into his thin chest, each breath gurgling until he started coughing and clasped a kerchief to his mouth. Although he held it tightly, Lewis saw the bright red blood soaking into the cloth along with older encrusted brown stains.

Lewis averted his eyes and waited for the coughing

to end, as did the other men. A minute passed until Maxwell got control of himself. Wayne broke the silence.

'Payment,' he said simply, holding out a hand.

'Are you worried,' Maxwell asked in a weak and reedy voice, 'I won't live for long enough to pay you?'

Wayne said nothing, but his firm set jaw suggested this was the case and so with a rueful grunt, Maxwell handed over an envelope. Then he dismissed them. Both men glanced at each other and then at Lewis before leaving.

As they walked away they muttered to each other. Before they went out of earshot to collect up the horses and bodies, Lewis heard enough to gather they thought neither man would live to see another sun-up.

Then Lewis waited quietly for Maxwell to begin. After all, he knew about revenge and how the avenger played it out.

The other men had ridden off into the gathering gloom when Maxwell finally fixed him with his watery gaze and spoke.

'Talk,' he said.

'I tried to talk four months ago,' Lewis said. 'My story won't change none from then. So get this over with while you still can.'

'I'll do this in my own time and I have time enough to hear it.' Maxwell gave a slight shrug of his thin shoulders. 'Perhaps last time I wasn't prepared to listen to what you had to say, so just say the words.'

Maxwell's grave tone gave Lewis no comfort that even if he were prepared to listen, it would change his intentions, but he did owe him an explanation. Lewis nodded towards the door.

'They threw my saddlebag over there. Get the second journal; it records everything that happened on that day.'

Maxwell narrowed his eyes, suggesting he thought this a trick, but when Lewis stayed quiet, he pried himself out of his chair and shuffled to the door. He looped a foot around the saddlebag then pushed it across the floor. He continued to kick the bag until he reached the chair where he flopped down on to it.

He took several deep breaths to get his strength back then picked up the bag. Cautiously he opened it, his steady movements giving the impression he reckoned a rattler might dart out, but all that was inside was a tied up block of journals, as promised.

'I never thought a killer like you would keep a diary,' he said.

'I'm not a killer. I'm a decent man.'

Maxwell snorted his breath, as if this were the last thing he wanted to hear. Then he riffled through the journals to extract the second one. He flicked through the dated pages until he reached the day that had come to control his life.

Then he read aloud.

Lewis had started his record of events to help him keep track of the conflicting rumours and snippets of information he gathered about Emerson Greeley.

As there was no essential information in the events of that day he had rarely looked at that part of his chronicle. So the words sounded unfamiliar, but the events they described were still fresh in his mind. . . .

It had happened in Foster's Pass, a small town similar to Liberty, a short drag with a mercantile and stables. Few people had been about, although a distinctive roan stood outside the saloon.

Lewis had looked out for the roan for the last two months and he would have recognized it anywhere. After all, it had been his until Emerson had stolen it.

He could have gone straight into the saloon and confronted Emerson, but he didn't want to give him any warning about his impending demise and so give him a chance to fight back. So he headed to the stables and, standing beneath the eaves in shadow, he waited.

An hour passed, then two. Sundown encouraged other men to go into the saloon from where the growing sounds of boisterous conversations emerged, but Emerson didn't come out.

Presently two boys ran into then out of the saloon, their laughter suggesting they'd won a dare by going inside. Then they headed towards the stables.

On the ground before him they played a game that involved rolling an old wagon wheel back and forth. To ensure they wouldn't get in the way of what was about to happen he called them over.

He gave the eldest a dime to tell him who was

inside the saloon. This didn't get him much information beyond the lad reporting that most of the men from the town were inside, but the promise of another coin got him the information that a man he didn't recognize was at the bar.

This was as good a description as Lewis could hope to get, as his own last sighting of Emerson had been brief and was two months old.

As he judged the boys competent he gave them both a dollar for their next task, a payment that concentrated their minds.

Then Lewis took advantage of the gathering darkness to make his circuitous way over to stand square on to the saloon doorway, ensuring he would immediately see anyone who came out. Even better, that person wouldn't be able to see well straight away when they emerged into the darkness from the well lit saloon.

The younger boy walked to the roan, unhitched it, then calmly led it away from the saloon.

The elder boy waited until his friend had followed Lewis's instructions of leaving it beside the stables then hurrying away. Then he ran into the saloon doorway.

'Someone's just made off with a horse!' he shouted, his voice cutting through the hubbub inside. 'It's this roan.'

Then he did as instructed and scampered into hiding to stay away from the trouble that was about to erupt.

Lewis didn't have to wait long for the result.

A man came barrelling out through the doorway, liquor making his gait uncertain, his hand rising to shield his eyes from stray light as he looked around for the stolen horse. He espied it by the stables and set off.

'Emerson Greeley?' Lewis called out, standing tall.

The man stopped just beyond the long rectangle of light cast through the door, his form shrouded in shadows. Then he turned.

That was all the proof Lewis needed. He fired, blasting the man in the chest.

The man staggered backwards for a pace then tumbled to the ground, landing with his face positioned in the light patch and letting Lewis see he'd made a terrible mistake.

The man wasn't Emerson Greeley.

He'd killed the wrong man, a man, as he was to learn later, called Raymond Templeton.

The remaining events of that day weren't detailed in the journal but the summation of them was that despite it being a mistake, his elder brother Maxwell couldn't accept Lewis's explanations.

'I thought your brother was Emerson Greeley,' Lewis said when Maxwell stopped reading. Then he repeated his last words to Maxwell from four months ago before he'd fled from a rapidly worsening situation. 'I'm sorry.'

'I don't want your apology,' Maxwell snapped, slamming shut the journal.

31

'I know, but the explanation I wrote there is the truth. As you'll see on the next page, I learnt later that Emerson had sold the horse to Raymond for a pittance that very day then made off. He didn't need the money so it must have been to put me off his trail, but I guess even he couldn't have expected that result.'

'He couldn't, unless he knew what a trigger-happy killer you are.'

'I'm not a killer.'

'The dead men you've strewn in your wake would suggest otherwise.'

Lewis sighed. 'I was a decent man married to a good woman and leading a quiet life in Fort Lord until Emerson took it all away, so I know how you feel. For what it's worth, to my mind your brother was as much a victim of Emerson's crime as I was, but I know you don't want to hear that. So just get this over with.'

Maxwell pointed a shaking finger at him. 'You do not know how I feel.'

Maxwell stood. He swayed before he got his balance then shuffled across the room towards him.

Although he'd steeled himself not to react Lewis tensed. He watched Maxwell's every pace then listened intently when he stepped behind him. Rustling sounded, then Maxwell lunged forward and a blindfold rasped as it slipped over Lewis's eyes.

'Is there anything you want to say,' Lewis said, sitting rigidly, 'Or for me to say before you kill me?'

'What can you say? Remorse? Regrets?' Maxwell

snorted as he stomped round to stand before Lewis. 'The only thing I want is for you to suffer.'

'I have.'

'Not because of what you did to my brother, but because of what Emerson Greeley did to you.'

Through the thin weave of the blindfold Lewis watched Maxwell back away from him. Then he jerked out of view, the thud of him hitting the wall sounding a moment later, followed by him slumping to the floor.

'Are you all right?' Lewis asked when he'd heard nothing but ragged breathing for a minute.

'I'm not well,' Maxwell murmured, his voice almost too low to hear.

'I know. If you let me go, I'll fetch help.'

Maxwell coughed weakly. 'I'm not letting you go, and nobody can help me. I've not got long.'

'How long?'

'They gave me a week two months ago, but I had something to live for.' A racking cough sounded. 'So I can wait for you to show some remorse.'

'All I can say is, every day I've thought of my mistake and I regret what I did to your brother.'

'That's not enough. So you'll have to do some suffering first.' Maxwell cleared his throat, the act inducing another round of hacking coughs.

Gradually the coughing petered out and Lewis sat tall waiting for the inevitable.

A gunshot blasted, the sound echoing in the small room.

Lewis tensed, expecting that Maxwell would fire again after his first shot had gone awry, but then he heard a thud, as of a body hitting the floor.

'Maxwell?' Lewis asked, but he received no answer. 'What have you done?'

He still didn't get an answer, but in the long hours that followed he came to understand what had happened and why.

The dying Maxwell had shot himself instead of shooting him. He had only a short time to live, perhaps hours, and his final comment provided the only clue as to why he had taken this unexpected action.

He hadn't been compassionate: he had wanted to make Lewis suffer. Abandoning him at a Flag station where nobody other than the weekly train ever visited ensured his death would be a slower and more painful one than the quick finality of the bullet he'd reserved for himself.

Lewis was determined not to suffer a lingering death, even if the tantalizing hope that Maxwell had given him was part of the suffering he had aimed to inflict.

When he was sure Maxwell was in fact dead he tested his bonds, but they were tight, holding his wrists and his ankles and securing them to the chair. So he'd have to find something to tear through the ropes.

Wayne and Snyder had rifled through his saddlebag and taken everything but his journals, leaving Maxwell as his only source of unintentional help. So he tipped himself over to lie on his side then a few inches at a time, he wormed his way across the room, finally reaching Maxwell's body.

He nudged the body with his head, rolling it over, then rubbed his head up and down against Maxwell's chest, the action removing the blindfold and letting him at least see his predicament.

Then he nuzzled through Maxwell's pockets searching for something he could use to free himself, but found nothing. And the hour he spent gathering up Maxwell's gun only proved that Maxwell had in fact brought only one bullet.

So he wormed his way to the doorway where he leaned back against the jamb. Propped there he looked around, seeing that neither Maxwell's mount nor his own was there, confirming that Maxwell had planned all along to act out his revenge in this manner.

Lewis looked at Maxwell's slumped body, shaking his head, then set about rubbing his wrists up and down the corner of the adobe wall. The wall crumbled and didn't provide much friction, but Lewis couldn't see anything else nearby that he could use.

He worked diligently until first light then through the day, stopping and trying to open his hands whenever his muscles protested. Each time nothing happened, and with his hands being held behind his back he couldn't tell if he was making progress.

35

He tried to use his weight to break the chair, but aside from creaking it was too resilient, and as the day grew warmer his thirst grew too, making him wonder if he should try to alleviate that need first. This thought made him remember the other bodies that had been out the back.

They had been taken away, but perhaps someone had dropped something he could use.

Lewis gave up on his attempts to free himself and, on his side, he snaked his way through the door. He cast a lingering glance at the water tower, filled with out of reach water, and at the pump that needed two men to operate. They were fifty yards away: even if he were able to drag himself there in the heat, there was little chance he'd be able to find succour.

He embarked on the long journey around the station. He picked the shaded side, but even so he was panting and sweat he couldn't afford to lose slicked his body by the time he edged himself around the back corner to see what was there.

He found nothing.

When he finally admitted defeat Lewis flopped to lie with his face pressed to the warm dirt, demoralized and resigned to his fate.

But then the resilience that had got him through six months of chasing after Emerson Greeley made him raise himself and wriggle across the ground until he could press himself to the wall. There the adobe wasn't so crumbled and there were even a few stones mixed in. He located a stone with his hands and began a sawing motion against it.

This time he found he couldn't work for as long as before and he had to take longer breaks before restarting.

Night provided coolness and some respite, but by then cramps in his arms and legs were bunching, then numbing his muscles, making it harder for him to move: his desperation was growing. The hope he'd had when he'd worked out what Maxwell had done no longer sustained him and he didn't think he could last another day.

If he didn't free himself by morning, he was doomed.

Despite his desperation, however, exhaustion made him fall into a fitful sleep.

Uneasy dreams flitted through his mind until he awoke with a start to hear the patter of hoofbeats approaching the station.

He listened with a mixture of hope and concern. He expected that one of the two men who'd taken him from Liberty had returned, but when the newcomer went into the station, the strangulated scream that tore out was a woman's.

'What's happened?' she cried out, her voice letting him identify her as Elizabeth Fisher, the woman who had tried to hire him two days ago to find her husband's killer.

'I'm out the back,' Lewis called, his voice emerging as a croak and forcing him to repeat the words.

Pattering footfalls sounded before she scooted around the side to look down at him.

'What? How?' she murmured.

'It's a long story,' Lewis said, now relieved, 'And I'll tell you about it, but you've got to free me first.'

She appraised his bonds then grabbed his chair and, with Lewis's help in rocking back and forth, she righted it. Then she turned on her heel and left him to go back into the station.

She returned with the other chair and set it before him.

'I'll free you,' she said. She sat and folded her arms then continued speaking, this time in a matter-of-fact manner. 'But first you have to agree to do something for me.'

Lewis winced. 'As I told you two days ago, I am not for hire. I will not track down the man who killed your husband.'

She shrugged, then looked to the eastern horizon.

'That's what you say now, but it'll be sun-up in a few hours and I reckon it won't be long before you'll agree to do anything I want.'

CHAPTER 4

The sun was at its highest, blasting down with incessant heat.

The shadow cast by the station still covered Lewis's bowed head, but it wouldn't do so for much longer and he doubted he could stay conscious once the sun was able to do its worst.

Since Elizabeth had found him he had picked at the ropes and wriggled his hands behind his back. A few hours ago he'd felt them give a little, but he hadn't felt them move again.

Now he was too weak to struggle any more.

Elizabeth was sitting facing him with a parasol over her shoulder shielding her face; a water bottle lay on her lap while she idly browsed through his journals.

They hadn't spoken since their initial exchange, but over the last hour she had frequently glanced at him and smiled, clearly judging they were approaching the

39

time when he would have to give in.

Lewis reckoned she was right.

'I'll pay you,' she said, as if she was just continuing their conversation from many hours ago.

'That makes your offer even worse,' Lewis croaked. 'I just did what I had to do to get Emerson Greeley. That was personal. What you want me to do isn't.'

'It is for me.'

Lewis raised his head to look at her. 'Then do it yourself.'

'I haven't got the skills.' She waved the journal. 'You have. You noted Emerson's details, put together the information you uncovered, and found him. That's what I need.'

'It's not what I need.'

'Then you'll die.' She shrugged, uttering a contented giggle that in other circumstances would have cheered him. 'Unless you say the words that you'll help me.'

Lewis stretched as far as he was able. The action gave him an odd feeling in his hands behind his back, but it made him smile. He had given up wriggling his hands but maybe now. . . .

'How do you know I won't just say the words to make you free me then go back on my promise?'

'Perhaps you will, but you'll say them first.'

Lewis jerked his head back, beckoning her to approach.

'Then come here and I'll say it, Elizabeth Fisher.'

She narrowed her eyes, noting his sudden change of mind, then stood. She put down the journal and the water bottle on the chair then walked over to him, twirling the parasol.

'Say it,' she said.

'Come closer.'

She leaned down.

'Say it,' she whispered.

Lewis shot a hand out from behind his back, the loosened ropes falling away from him, grabbed her wrist, then dragged her down to his eye level.

'I am not for hire,' he rasped into her face, then shoved her away and got to his feet.

He tried to stand with dignity but his bound and cramped legs forced him to sway and his desperate need for water was too great. He bounded over to the water bottle, unplugged it, then dropped to his knees and threw enough water down his throat to make him choke. Then he rolled round to sit and tore at his bonds.

'I wouldn't have let you die,' she said, with a tremor of fear in her voice as she backed away to stand against the wall.

'I know.' He looked up as he looped away the last of the ropes. 'If it helps, if I thought you would, I'd have said the words.'

'Then helped me?'

'Nope,' he said, standing.

'But you have to,' she pleaded. She walked over to stand before him. 'You're the only man who can.'

Lewis took another slug of water. 'Plenty of men will do what you want me to do for money.'

'I know, but I've spent a long time finding you. I don't want to start searching again.'

'Then don't. Go back home. Start a new life. Forget about revenge.'

'I can't,' she snapped, her eyes flaring with an anger Lewis had experienced many times himself. 'I want him to suffer.'

Lewis snorted then set off walking towards Liberty.

'Someone else said that to me recently,' he called over his shoulder. 'Except the only person who suffered was him, and it'll be the same for you.'

'And you?'

'I sure did.' Lewis stopped and turned. 'But my suffering's ended and I'm not going down that path again. I'm sorry, but I won't kill a man for you.'

She provided a resigned shrug. 'Then if you won't help me, Lewis Coltaine, where will you go and what will you do?'

Lewis considered for a moment then smiled.

'Maybe,' he said, 'I'll take my own advice, Elizabeth Fisher.'

'You can't stop me going in there,' Harlan Coltaine said.

Cameron sighed as he dismounted. 'I can't, but it'll be better if you stayed here and left me to do the talking.'

'Talking!' Harlan glanced at his own gun, then at

42

Cameron's. 'We're packing six-shooters for the first time in years and you claim we're here to talk!'

Cameron snorted a harsh laugh. 'Armed or not, the important thing is that we get to the truth.'

Harlan's sneer suggested he thought getting the truth from the Miller brothers was unlikely and Cameron had to agree.

The last few days had been difficult.

Marshal Ingersoll had questioned everyone in White Creek and tracked down a few who had just passed through, but everyone had given him the same answer. Nobody had seen anything, nobody had seen anyone acting suspiciously near the Coltaine house and nobody had any real suspicions as to why anyone would want to kill Jesse.

The people who had been in town for years and knew of the history between the Coltaine family and the Miller brothers had aired a few views, but they couldn't provide anything of substance.

The brothers themselves had been their usual uncooperative selves, but from the sightings Ingersoll had pieced together of their movements, he'd concluded they hadn't been near the Coltaine house.

Cameron and Harlan weren't prepared to accept that; with Jesse now buried, as they had promised, they stood outside the Millers' trading post, ten miles out of White Ridge.

With Harlan doing as requested and standing by his horse, Cameron headed to the door, but before he reached it Ward Miller emerged, a rifle in hand.

'Get off my land, Coltaine,' he muttered, eyeing him with cold menace and contempt.

Over his shoulder in the post, Cameron could see the elder brother Jacob lurking around, also brandishing a rifle.

'Surprised you're managing to hold a gun,' Cameron said, noting with a wry smile that this was the first time he'd spoken to either of the two elder Miller brothers in ten years. 'This late in the day it's usually a bottle.'

Ward's eyes flared as he thrust the rifle up to his shoulder to take aim at Cameron.

'I've taken just about as many insults as I can stomach from you. Leave while you can still ride away.'

Cameron clenched his fists, an angry oath hovering on his lips, but his own earlier comment came back to him and he forced himself to remain calm.

'I haven't insulted you that I remember. But after we had to bury our brother we have some questions. Oblige us with the answers and we'll go.'

'We did all our talking to the lawman. Ask him.'

'We have. Now I'm asking you.' Cameron paused, giving Ward time to answer, although his sneer said he wouldn't be taking up the offer. 'Do you know anything about Jesse's death? Have you heard of Mason Crockett?'

The last question made Ward flinch, at least

confirming the name was familiar to him.

'Why should I talk to you when you at least got to plant your brother?'

Cameron leaned forward, pleased that Ward's responses, both verbally and unconsciously made, confirmed they had been right; that Jesse's death was related to the source of the feud between the two families.

'Jesse killed your brother twelve years ago, but then again he deserved everything he got. Jesse didn't deserve nothing in return.'

'Yeah, it was twelve years ago, but you rotten Coltaines won't leave him alone, will you?'

'I don't know what you mean.'

Ward ground his teeth then firmed his arm, the rifle swinging up to take steady aim at Cameron's head, but from behind him he heard a click, then steady footfalls.

'If that finger tightens a hair's breadth more,' Harlan said, 'I'll blow you and your worthless brother to hell.'

Ward darted his gaze past Cameron's shoulder and what he saw there made his right eye twitch.

'It never changes,' he muttered. 'The Coltaines are still riding on to Miller land with guns and threats.'

'We didn't start those threats,' Cameron said. 'We just want some answers.'

'That's what Jesse Coltaine said the last time.' Ward kept the gun on him for a moment longer,

45

then sighed and lowered it. 'But if you want some answers, come with me.'

Ward stared at Harlan until he lowered his gun and then, with the rifle dangling from one hand, he grabbed Cameron's arm and moved to march him away from the door.

Cameron dug his heels in until Ward loosened his grip. Then he followed him with Harlan trailing behind. They went around the post to the back and paced away up a short rise.

At the top of the rise there was a weed-infested area in which a picket fence had once marked out a square, but long ago that fence had fallen over and now lay mouldered. Only the mounds within explained what this area had once been.

Cameron walked forward and because he knew what to look for, he could make out the names of Baxter and Sarah – Ward's parents – etched into flat, split rocks. The work had been done at a time when the Miller brothers still had pride in themselves and so it had stood the test of time.

Cameron couldn't work out what Ward had brought him here to see and as he said nothing else, he walked towards the mounds. The land beyond the two graves became visible. Like the Coltaine plot there were small mounds for the unfortunate babies, but what drew his attention was the hole with earth piled at the side.

He had come here only once before, but casting his mind back he was sure who should be there.

Cameron swirled round to face Ward.

'Stacy?' he asked.

'That didn't sound like no guess to me,' Ward grunted.

'It wasn't. I remembered. . . .' Cameron turned away then paced closer to the hole and ventured a glance inside.

It was empty.

He beckoned for Harlan to approach.

'What's this mean, Cameron?' Harlan asked when he joined him in looking into the empty grave. His question gathered a snort of derision from Ward.

'I don't know,' Cameron said, 'but I reckon Ward's showing us that someone's violated their brother's grave.'

'*Someone* has,' Ward said. 'It wasn't enough that you had to kill him, you then had to dig him up. Why did you do it? Where did you take him?'

Cameron shook his head, this unexpected discovery taking him aback and making him speechless, but Harlan spoke up.

'It wasn't us,' he said, his softer voice betraying his own emotions. 'When did this happen?'

Ward sneered, as if they should know the answer to that question.

'Six, seven months ago. We weren't too sure. We . . . we were busy at the time.'

Cameron firmed his jaw to avoid making a sarcastic comment about how their usual drunken

47

state had probably stopped them noticing.

'And is the missing body the reason why you killed Jesse?'

Ward's face reddened. Then he advanced on Harlan and swung the rifle up to aim it at his stomach.

'I'm not standing for no more of your questions and threats. You've got one minute to get off our land or I will blast you both in two.'

Harlan's hand twitched towards his holster, but before he could test if Ward was bluffing, Cameron slapped a hand on his shoulder and gripped it tightly.

'Come on,' he said. 'We've got all the answers we'll get today.'

Harlan glared at Ward for a few moments longer, then backed away.

'Don't go thinking that this is over,' he said, then before Ward could retort he turned on his heel and headed back to his horse.

Neither man looked back and neither did they discuss what had happened until they were approaching their own house.

'What you reckon?' Cameron asked, breaking the silence.

'I reckon I got it right back there,' Harlan said. 'Someone dug up Stacy's body. The Millers brooded and got themselves all worked up about it until they shot Jesse in retaliation.'

'It's possible, but the thought on my mind is why

would someone, perhaps this Mason Crockett, dig up his body in the first place?'

Harlan shrugged as he drew his horse to a halt.

'It might not have been our mystery man. It could have been Ward in a drunken stupor and he forgot about it when he sobered up.'

Cameron nodded then dismounted. He noted that a horse he hadn't seen before was in their small corral at the side of the house.

'We taking this information to Ingersoll?'

'Sure.' Harlan dismounted and followed Cameron. 'We promised him we would, but if he doesn't act, what we do afterwards is up to us.'

Cameron stopped at the door and turned.

'You saying what I think you're saying?'

'Sure. Jesse had the right idea about Stacy twelve years ago and that's still the only behaviour the Miller brothers understand. So we do whatever we have to do to get to the truth.'

Cameron shook his head. 'We don't. There could be more going on here than we first thought. Until we know more, we're not dragging the Miller brothers out in the dead of night for no summary justice.'

Harlan snorted, his firm set jaw suggesting he'd argue, but with a rueful nod he accepted he'd spoken in anger.

'All right,' he said. He lightened his tone as he opened the door and went inside. 'I'll do whatever my eldest brother says I have to do.'

49

Then Harlan came to a sudden halt and a moment later a familiar voice spoke up from inside.

'If you want someone to tell you what to do,' the voice said, 'then you should listen to your real eldest brother.'

Cameron pushed past Harlan to see that Mary and Esther were sitting by the fireplace looking at a man standing by the window: Lewis Coltaine.

'We don't see you in ten years,' Cameron snapped, 'and then this week of all weeks you just happen to ride into town.'

'Listen to what he has to say, Cameron,' Mary said, 'before you say something you'll regret.'

Cameron acknowledged her request with a firm nod then considered Lewis, raising his eyebrows in an invitation for him to speak.

'I came to visit and heard the news,' Lewis said. 'I weren't exactly Jesse's favourite brother, but I'll pay my respects.'

'Have you even bothered,' Harlan said, 'to ask what happened to him?'

Lewis rubbed his jaw before he spoke.

'Mary's explained,' he said lightly, as if he were just discussing the weather. 'You got any idea who was responsible?'

Cameron looked Lewis up and down, noting that despite him sitting in the safe environment of the family home he was packing a gun.

'Maybe,' he said.

CHAPTER 5

Lewis stood over Jesse's fresh grave searching for a feeling inside, but he felt nothing. They'd let him come out here alone, probably because they knew of his opinion about Jesse.

The last time he'd seen his brother they had argued, as they always had, and the passage of time hadn't dimmed the hostility. So no sorrowful thoughts came and the brooding desire for revenge that had consumed him for the last six months didn't overcome him either.

With no other purpose in mind after killing Emerson, he'd felt that coming here was the right thing to do to start his life afresh.

Despite his antipathy, the news of Jesse's murder had shocked him, but only because it made him wonder whether Emerson's final taunt could have been genuine after all. Perhaps someone had been hired to destroy the contented lives of the Coltaines, but he'd dismissed the idea as too unlikely: the events had happened too far apart in time and location.

But one thing was clear already: there was nothing for him here and he wouldn't be restarting that life back at the family home. Perhaps some wounds are too deep to be overcome even at times like this, he decided.

He looked up to see that Cameron was making his slow way over to him from the house, a sight that pleased Lewis as it meant he wouldn't have to go back inside.

'Are you staying?' Cameron asked in a low tone that said he expected only a negative answer.

'Take that worried look off your face, brother. I'm leaving.'

Cameron sighed. 'By rights a quarter . . . a third of everything here is yours. At the very least you could stay the night to stop you looking for somewhere to sleep. We've got room for two.'

'Two?' Lewis sighed then looked aloft as he realized that meant Elizabeth hadn't taken his hint to stay back, just like she'd ignored his demands to stop following him. 'She's not with me. She's been trailing me, not listening to sense. Don't let her in the house.'

Cameron smiled. 'This time you're the one who can take the worried look off his face. Harlan spoke with her and she wasn't enthused about coming inside.'

'Then that makes two of us.' Lewis moved to go,

but Cameron stepped to the side to block his way.

'You were right. You and Jesse hated each other and at a time like this, we don't want to be reminded of that. But we have a family decision to make and while you're here, I'd welcome hearing your perspective.'

Lewis noted it would get dark soon.

'All right,' he said with a resigned sigh, 'but just for the one night. Then I'm moving on.'

'This could be down to bad luck with a low-life being up to no good,' Harlan said. While walking back and forth before the fire he punctuated his points with a slap of a fist against palm. 'Or it's the Miller brothers finally getting revenge because of Stacy's demise. Or it's someone else who has a grudge against Jesse.'

Cameron uttered a supportive grunt. Then all eyes turned to Lewis.

Earlier, Mary had fed him a heel of bread and a chunk of cheese. He leaned back in his chair then tore off a mouthful of each.

'Why are you looking at me?' he asked, spluttering crumbs.

'Because you're staying,' Cameron said, 'to give us your opinion.'

Lewis shrugged. 'If those are the choices, I'll opt for it being bad luck. Plenty of terrible things happen in this world. People killing the wrong man and suchlike.'

Harlan and Cameron glanced at each other. Then

Cameron coughed before he spoke up.

'Ever hear of Mason Crockett?' he said.

Lewis considered. He'd kept his journals to help him make sense of the conflicting information he'd received, but even so, he was good at remembering names.

'Nope,' he said, then gnawed off another mouthful.

'Then do you know of anyone who has a grudge against Jesse?'

Lewis considered Cameron's blank and guarded expression.

'So that's what Harlan meant when he said *someone* else.' Lewis munched through the last mouthful. 'But the answer's no. I would never have hurt him. So you should consider if there are others who have a grudge against him. He killed Stacy Miller and if he could do that, then he—'

'Be quiet!' Harlan shouted, jumping to his feet so quickly he tipped over his chair. 'You're not dirtying Jesse's good name.'

'He's not got a good name.'

Harlan pointed a firm finger at him. 'He was a fine man and he hated you, so what does that make you?'

Lewis didn't react other than to pick crumbs off the table. It was left to Cameron to stand up and place his hands on Harlan's shoulders to calm him down.

'Enough,' he said. 'We have to talk this through rationally.'

54

'That's what we were doing until he said those things about Jesse.'

Cameron kept his hands gripped tightly until Harlan provided a brief nod and muttered that he'd calmed down. Then he turned to Lewis.

'Have you got anything to say,' he said, 'that don't involve maligning someone who can't be here to speak for himself?'

'And have you got anything to say,' Lewis said, 'that don't involve maligning me because I didn't like a dead man?'

'Just answer the damn question!' Harlan roared before Cameron could answer, his face reddening.

The two men glared at each other, leaving Cameron to interject.

'This is getting us nowhere,' he snapped.

Harlan muttered an oath under his breath then took a long pace towards Lewis, his fists bunching. But just when he looked as if he'd confront him he turned on his heel. He stormed outside and slammed the door behind him so firmly it rebounded open and swung back and forth letting everyone see him pace away.

Everyone remained quiet and avoided looking at each other until Mary went over to Cameron and placed a hand on his shoulder.

'Go after him,' she said.

Cameron nodded and after a quick glare at Lewis, he followed Harlan out.

Silence reigned for a minute until Lewis spoke up.

'Well,' he said with laughter in his tone, 'they can't hate me that much if they've left me alone with their womenfolk.'

Cameron leaned on the bar beside Harlan.

Jackson McGiven, the bartender, moved to pour him a whiskey, but Cameron told him to leave the bottle. He poured himself a glassful and topped up Harlan's glass.

Harlan swirled his glass, considering the liquor.

'I've had enough,' he said, then placed the glass down.

'Perhaps you have,' Cameron said, 'but we don't get to come here too often these days. Make the most of it.'

Harlan laughed, then took a sip. 'Perhaps you're right, and I'm sorry. I had to get away before I said something.'

'Only said? I thought you were going to hit him.' Cameron took a gulp of whiskey as Harlan grunted that this was the case.

'I know he and Jesse didn't get on, but even if he is my brother, I can't be civil to him until Jesse's death makes him feel something.'

'I know what you mean,' Cameron said with a heavy sigh. 'Has coming here helped any?'

'Not yet. I still can't get it clear in my mind whether it has something to do with the Miller brothers or Mason Crockett.'

The mentioning of the last name made a patron

who had been hunched over further down the bar look up. Cameron saw that it was Thomas Miller, the youngest and most responsible of the brothers.

Although from the way Thomas staggered backwards and had to throw out a hand to grab the bar to stop himself falling, Cameron reckoned he was acting in a manner that was more traditional for a Miller. He also noted Thomas was packing a gun.

Thomas lurched away from the bar then made his uncertain way over to them. Cameron's interest in him made Harlan turn.

'What you saying?' Thomas said, slurring his words.

'We're trying to work out who killed Jesse,' Cameron said. 'Maybe your reaction says you know something.'

'And what if I do?' Thomas said, taking a staggered pace towards him. He stabbed a finger at Cameron's chest, but his ill-judged motion in his drunken state made the hand veer away and brush past Cameron's right shoulder. 'What good will it do you? Do you want to end up dead too?'

'What you trying to tell us, Thomas?'

'Mason Crockett is what I'm saying, but forget that name. It's death to anyone who utters it.'

Thomas put a finger to his lips in an exaggerated gesture, urging them to be silent. Then he waved a dismissive hand at them and moved to head to the door, but Cameron slapped a hand on his shoulder, halting him.

'Who is he?' he asked.

Sudden rage contorted Thomas's face before he threw Cameron's hand off him. Then he pushed him away to make him sprawl over the bar and embarked on a snaking route to the door.

'Wait!' Harlan said, hurrying after him.

Thomas spun round and, despite his inebriated state, his hand flew with unerring accuracy to his holster. He drew his gun, the action creating sudden quiet in the previously lively saloon room.

'Don't come no closer,' he ordered. 'I can defend myself.'

Harlan hunched his shoulders, glaring at him and suggesting he might test whether that was true, so Cameron pushed himself away from the bar and joined Harlan, but he kept his hands held high.

'We came here for a quiet drink and neither of us is armed,' he said. 'So just go and sleep this off.'

'How can I sleep it off? It's all my fault. I did it. I did it all, and now I'm going to pay.'

Thomas's gunhand shook, his eyes rolled, and for a terrible moment it looked as if the distressed man would fire, but then he lowered his gun and tried to slot it into his holster. The gun missed by several inches and after twice brushing it down his leg, he gave up and turned on his heel. With the gun thrust high he lurched through the batwings to disappear into the night.

Harlan looked at Cameron, his mouth open in surprise.

'Did he just admit to killing Jesse?' he asked.

'I'm not sure,' Cameron said. 'But I reckon at the very least he knows who did do it.'

'Then we have to go after him.'

'Not when he's in that state. This time, I reckon we do what we were asked to do and take it to Ingersoll. He can work out what's been going on here.'

CHAPTER 6

They were discussing him in the main room.

Since first light Cameron and Harlan had been talking animatedly while their wives fed Lewis's nephews and nieces. For most of the time, lying on the floor in what had been Jesse's room, Lewis had been able to hear every word, but now they were talking quietly.

Lewis stretched, went to the window and searched the horizon for his unwelcome shadow, but she wasn't there.

In an odd way that disquieted him and in a pensive mood he headed into the main room. His arrival generated a sudden quietness and with all eyes on him, he sat at the table and considered them.

Cameron and Harlan were sitting by the fire with Esther and Mary, their folded arms and angled postures suggesting they had been disagreeing about something.

Esther got to her feet and poured Lewis a coffee then presented him with a mess of congealed beans and a thick hunk of bread.

Lewis gave her a beaming smile that made Harlan cast a surly glare at him. Then he started eating, savouring his food in the way only a man who didn't know when he'd next eat could.

'The way I see it,' Harlan said. He coughed and shuffled on his chair, suggesting that whatever he was about to say wasn't picking up from where the debate had ended. 'Marshal Ingersoll has to arrest Thomas.'

'What's happened?' Lewis asked before Cameron could reply.

'You're not interested,' Harlan snapped.

'Just pretend that I am and tell me.'

Harlan didn't reply, leaving Cameron to speak up and describe the odd encounter the previous night with Thomas Miller, which they'd left Ingersoll to follow up.

With Lewis having nothing to say about the matter, his revelation initiated several minutes of silence, broken only by the sounds of him munching his meal.

Presently hoofbeats closed outside.

Cameron looked through the window and reported that Ingersoll had arrived before returning to being silent.

When the door opened Ingersoll gave Lewis a brief look that didn't register any surprise then turned to Cameron.

'I'd heard he was back,' he said, jerking a thumb at Lewis.

'How?' Cameron asked. 'We didn't mention it.'

'I've been out to the Miller trading post. Elizabeth Fisher is staying there.' Ingersoll purposefully turned his back on Lewis. 'And it pains me to say this, but you ignored my orders.'

Cameron frowned. 'We went out to the post, but it weren't to cause trouble.'

'Except even when you're avoiding trouble, you've nearly got into fights with the Miller brothers twice. So I've got to ask you, are you two calm enough to listen to what's happened?'

'Sure,' Cameron said.

'What you learnt?' Harlan demanded, leaping to his feet and belying Cameron's promise.

Ingersoll didn't reply for several seconds, his stern expression making Harlan mumble an apology, then sit down.

'Stacy's not the only Miller who's gone missing. Thomas hightailed it out of town last night, heading west. He's the only lead I have about the killing and he's also my only suspect, so I'm going after him and I could do with some help.'

'We'll come,' Harlan said as Cameron murmured his own support.

'But I don't want no repeat of what happened to Stacy twelve years ago,' Ingersoll said. 'So you'll work to my rules.'

'We will,' Cameron said. 'And we're obliged you're letting us help.'

'Don't be. I just figured that if you're with me I can

watch you and stop you going after him on your own.'

Cameron acknowledged the sense of this attitude with a rueful smile then turned to Lewis.

'I guess you have the right to come with us.'

Lewis swallowed the last chunk of bread then shook his head.

'Last night Harlan nearly accused me of killing Jesse and yet now you want me to join you on a manhunt?'

'I didn't say that, but as Jesse's brother you've got the right to come along.'

Lewis didn't need to consider the offer, but he paused, ensuring he had everyone's attention before he replied.

'I vowed never to go on another Coltaine manhunt,' he said. 'And besides, as I said last night, I'm just passing through.'

Ingersoll nodded, understanding what was on Lewis's mind, but Harlan muttered an oath, leaving Cameron to reply for them both.

'Then see that you do just pass through,' he said. 'We're leaving within the hour and so will you. Then, no matter what your reasoning, your lack of interest in this means none of us ever wants to see you again.'

'Why do your brothers hate you?' Mary asked.

Lewis stopped before the door and looked over his shoulder. He'd collected his belongings and had aimed to leave quietly now that Cameron and Harlan had gone, but Cameron's wife had other ideas. He noted that a smile was on her lips, so he returned one of his own.

'I was born wicked,' he said.

'I've seen no sign of that, but it doesn't appear as if I'll get the chance to know you now.' She patted her legs, then stood. 'But I won't have you roaming around saying bad things about my hospitality.'

She went over to the table and returned with a folded bundle. From within the enticing smell of warm bread emerged.

Lewis took the bundle. 'This'll taste just fine wherever I happen to lay my head down tonight.'

'Will it be with Elizabeth? I only saw her from a distance, but she looked nice.'

'It won't,' Lewis snapped then considered and softened his tone. 'I'm sure she is nice. That's why I'd be obliged if you don't tell her I've gone.'

Lewis tipped his hat and moved for the door, but Mary coughed making him turn back.

'Cameron and Harlan have gone, so you've got the time to answer one question, surely.'

'I have, as long as it's not about all the wicked things I did to make my brothers hate me.'

'It's not. What happened between Jesse and Stacy?'

'You've been in the family for a few years. You must know.'

'I've heard the official family story. I'd like to hear yours.' She smiled then gestured at the stove. 'I've

64

got a coffee ready – that'll fortify you for your journey.'

The story wasn't one he liked to recall and he did want to move on, but his brothers wouldn't be back for days and the smell of coffee was enticing. So he nodded, put down his saddlebag and joined her at the table.

'It'd take more than one coffee to tell the whole tale,' he said, still unsure whether he wanted to discuss this. But having spoken the words came easily. 'When Baxter Miller and Miles Coltaine set up here they got on fine, but they fell out. It didn't help when they both produced sons who were always fighting.'

'I can imagine,' she said with an encouraging smile as she poured two coffees.

'The big trouble came with the sisters. We had one apiece and when our parents died, the brothers became protective. That didn't stop Jesse taking a shine to Abigail Miller. He fought every one of her brothers to see her, and it might have worked out fine, but she got sick and died.'

'I didn't know that.' She put a hand to her mouth. 'That must be why he never married.'

'I guess.' Lewis fingered his mug, enjoying the warmth. 'He was never the same again. So when Stacy got close to our Delores, he became obsessively protective.'

'They never speak of her.'

Lewis nodded. 'I'm not surprised. One day Jesse and Stacy argued and Jesse ran him out of town.

Delores got so distressed she collapsed and had a miscarriage.'

'His?'

'Sure. Although none of us knew she was pregnant, idiots that we were. That was too much for Jesse. He claimed Stacy had been beating her. . . . It was probably untrue, but either way, he vowed to make him pay. I was worried he'd overreact, so I joined him on the first Coltaine manhunt.'

'So you had a hand in it,' she said, her tone sounding aggrieved for the first time.

'Not in that way. I told him to let them live their own lives, but he wouldn't listen. After two days of arguing he abandoned me.' Lewis sighed. 'He returned home three days later. He'd killed Stacy. He buried the body and wouldn't let the Millers know where for a year. We didn't have much in the way of the law in those days, so that ended the matter.'

'And what happened to Delores?'

'She couldn't forgive Jesse for killing Stacy. She left home. None of us saw her again.'

She considered him. 'And unlike Cameron and Harlan you never forgave Jesse for driving her away, did you?'

Lewis sipped his coffee to give himself time to collect his thoughts. He wasn't sure whether he hated him more for murdering Stacy or for the effect it'd had on Delores, but he was sure of one thing.

'I didn't. I enjoyed having a sister around. There

are two sides to every story, but I didn't like how Cameron's and Harlan's dislike for the Millers let them forgive Jesse.' He leaned over his coffee then looked up at her. 'So after Delores had gone we kept on arguing. In the end I left too.'

'And ten years wasn't long enough to stop the arguing.' She smiled. 'But it'd be good to know what happened to her. Why don't you find her? It sounds as if you were her favourite brother.'

'If she'd have wanted to be found, she'd have made the effort to contact someone by now.'

'And you're going to join her, aren't you, in leaving and not coming back?'

He took a last gulp of his coffee then stood.

'Yup.'

'And is there nobody out there for you?'

'There was once.' Lewis picked up his bag and this time Mary didn't stop him from leaving.

At a steady pace, Lewis headed north.

Only when he was a few miles along the trail did it occur to him that by going this way, he would pass by the Millers' trading post.

He had hoped to ride away without Elizabeth discovering that he'd left and certainly without giving her a way to work out where he'd gone. So he was minded to seek an alternate route, but for some reason he couldn't fathom, he kept on riding.

Only when he was outside the post did he stop.

Elizabeth's horse was in the corral at the side and

he considered it, wondering whether he could still ride on by.

He dismounted anyhow.

'You're a fool,' he said to himself as he headed into the post.

He went to the counter. Nobody emerged to see what he wanted so he slapped a hand on the counter with an insistent rhythm until Ward Miller wandered in from a side room, bleary-eyed and stooped.

'I'm coming,' he muttered. 'And you'd better make this worth my while.'

Lewis snorted a laugh. 'I see service hasn't improved none in the last ten years.'

Ward stomped to a halt, his eyes opening wide in surprise as he recognized his customer.

'I don't see a Coltaine in years and now they all come here stinking up the place.'

Lewis sniffed. 'Even my brothers couldn't make this place smell any worse.'

'Don't you go thinking that just because they ran you out of town ten years ago that you're any more welcome here than they are.'

'And don't you go thinking that just because you scared my brothers off you can do the same to me.'

Lewis fixed Ward with his cold gaze until he looked away.

'What you want, Coltaine?'

'Marshal Ingersoll and my brothers have ridden off after your Thomas. They've got it into their heads that he killed Jesse. I figure you probably didn't talk to them, but if there's something you want to say, you might talk to me.'

'So you can join them in getting Thomas?'

'Nope. I'm leaving town, but not with them.' Lewis shrugged. 'I just want to know.'

Ward firmed his jaw, looking as if he wouldn't answer then sighed and shuffled behind the counter. He leaned on it facing Lewis.

'When Jesse killed Stacy, Thomas was too young to understand, but last year he started asking questions. So we told him. Afterwards he visited Redemption where Jesse caught up with him to try to piece together the full story. He came back mighty worried. Then Stacy got dug up, Jesse got shot, and Thomas hightailed it out of town.'

'So you reckon he killed Jesse?'

'Or uncovered something that meant he feared for his life.'

'About this Mason Crockett?'

'Maybe.' Ward raised himself. 'So, have you got enough answers to leave me in peace?'

Lewis had only wanted to hear confirmation that whatever had happened to Jesse wasn't connected to Emerson Greeley's taunt. Although Ward didn't know the full story, he'd heard enough.

'Sure. I'll go just as soon as your guest is ready to leave.'

'Guest?' Ward narrowed his eyes. 'You mean Elizabeth Fisher?'

'Yup.'

'Then she's not leaving. I'm kicking her out. No woman who's been with a—' Ward screeched when Lewis grabbed his jaw then dragged his head down to the counter.

Calmly he yanked Ward's head to the side to lay his cheek on the wood. Then he drew his gun and pressed the barrel down against Ward's temple, buckling the skin.

'I told you, Ward,' he said leaning down so that his hot breath rustled Ward's sparse hair, 'I'm not like my brothers. I've killed eight men and the only thing stopping me killing the ninth and tenth is the fact I'd hate to please my brothers.'

Ward gulped. 'Just get her out of here.'

'Being as you asked so nicely.'

Lewis raised the gun then released his hold and pushed Ward away. He turned, but it was to face Elizabeth, standing in the entrance to a short corridor.

'I knew,' she said, 'when you said you'd had enough of killing that you were lying.'

'I didn't lie. I do what I have to do, which doesn't include doing what you say.'

'Either way, you've come for me.'

'I didn't say that either. I just hate the thought of a decent woman being forced to stay at the Millers' trading post.'

'Decent woman?' She smiled as she turned to go back to her room. 'That's a start.'

Lewis stayed for long enough to give Ward a

warning glare then followed her.

As it turned out, the room in which she had been staying was nothing like what he had expected. It was neat, books were on shelves, and the smell of neglect in the main post area hadn't permeated this part of the building.

'If I'd have known you were staying in comfort,' he said, 'I wouldn't have bothered rescuing you.'

'They let me stay in their younger brother's room,' she said as she placed a saddlebag on the bed. 'He reads a lot.'

While she collected her belongings then folded and placed them in the saddlebag Lewis went over to the bookshelves. He idly ran his finger along the line of books.

'Now that he's running for his life I hope that whatever he's learnt from these can help him keep one step ahead of my brothers.'

'And what about us? Where are we going?'

'*We* are going nowhere. I'm going somewhere and you're following me until you get bored and go somewhere else.'

She paused from her packing to laugh. 'And where are *you* going?'

'Don't know where it'll be, but it's more like a person than a place.'

She smiled. 'You're going on another manhunt?'

'I never said it was no man.'

This comment made her breathe deeply before she began slapping the rest of her belongings into the bag with greater speed. Then she rattled it closed and swung the bag over a shoulder.

'Come on, then. If you don't leave, I can't follow you.'

Lewis turned to go, but the open book sitting on the desk beneath the shelves caught his attention.

'You enjoy that?' he asked.

She shook her head. 'Not me. Thomas must have been reading it before I moved in.'

'Samuel Pepys's diary,' Lewis said, reading the title.

He picked up the book, his curiosity having been tweaked. Although he no longer needed to record his activities, he'd still written down his movements this morning. And here was a man who had clearly recorded his life for longer than he had.

Lewis thumbed through the pages until he found a bookmark. Then he read the last section Thomas would have read. It contained nothing of interest and so Lewis was about to close the book, but then the bookmark itself caught his attention.

Written down the centre was a single word: *Liberty*.

This was such a surprising thing to read that at first it didn't register. He read it again, confirming he was right, then had to throw out a hand to grab a shelf to stop himself swaying from the shock.

'What's wrong?' Elizabeth asked.

Lewis crunched up the bookmark, threw the book back on the desk, and breezed past her. He heard her hurrying after him, but he paid neither her nor the cringing Ward heed as he stormed through the post and outside.

When he reached his horse he again read the bookmark to confirm in the stronger light that he hadn't misread. He hadn't.

Thomas, a man who might have killed his brother, had written 'Liberty', the town where Lewis had killed Emerson Greeley, on a bookmark before he'd hightailed it out of town.

No matter how Lewis looked at it, that couldn't have been a coincidence; it plunged him straight back into hell.

CHAPTER 7

'What was in that book?' Elizabeth asked.

Lewis looked up from his studious consideration of their campfire.

'Stop prying,' he snapped.

'I only want to know what's worrying you. You were cheerful when you rescued me from the post, but since you opened that book, you've been distant.'

'It happens when you lose someone.'

'I know.' She leaned forward to throw a branch on the fire, sending sparks rippling up into the night sky. When she spoke again her voice was softer. 'Tell me about your wife.'

Lewis stared at the flames. He had bottled up his thoughts about what had happened, so he reckoned he didn't need to talk about it, but to his surprise words came tumbling out.

'I loved her, except I can't remember how that felt now. All I can remember is hearing a gunshot, then running to the barn and finding her dead body.'

'That must have been terrible.'

'Sure.' He gulped, then took a deep breath before continuing. 'For the last six months I'd hoped that when I'd killed Emerson Greeley I'd forget her lying there and remember the good times. And I might have done, but not now, not after opening that book and seeing Liberty written down.'

'The town where you caught up with Emerson?' she said, her voice catching and making her cough. She waited until Lewis nodded. 'Why would Thomas be interested in that place?'

'He must have worked out that Emerson is connected to Jesse's death. Why else would he have left town heading west, going towards the town I left last week?'

She rocked her head from side to side as she considered.

'I don't know, but neither can I see how what happened in Liberty can be connected to what happened in White Creek.'

'Neither can I, and that's what worries me the most.'

She smiled. 'I didn't think you were a man who worried.'

'As I've said, I'm not the man you want me to be.'

'Is that another way of telling me that you're still not interested in my offer?'

Lewis snorted then leaned forward to poke the fire with a stick.

'I wasn't interested when you asked me, I'm not

interested now, and I never will be.'

'Never is a long time.'

'It is, and if you stay with me, you'll see that when I said never, I meant it.' He threw the stick in the fire then looked at her through the flames. 'I don't know where this journey will take me. I have to find Thomas and find out why Liberty interested him. Then I have another journey in mind, and I have no idea when that'll start and when it'll end.'

'And that journey is to find this woman?'

Lewis again noted the disgruntled look she gave him at the thought of him trying to find a woman. He was minded to mention that the woman was his sister, but he also reckoned Elizabeth was starting to convince herself that she should leave him alone.

'Yeah,' he said.

'And there's no place for me in those plans?'

'There isn't, and I know you don't want to hear this, but believe me, vengeance is a cold duty that doesn't keep you warm at night. You need to move on and forget about it.'

She sighed and then moved over to her blanket.

'That's a fine piece of advice coming from a man who's on a manhunt because of a word he read in a book.'

Lewis didn't reply, figuring he'd said enough for now. He settled down under his blanket and tried to will himself to sleep.

He didn't expect it to work, but he quickly fell into a dreamless sleep and, as it turned out, he didn't get another chance to convince her to move on.

When he awoke in the morning she had gone.

Lewis prided himself on being alert even when asleep, so her success in leaving without rousing him perturbed him. Feeling in an unsettled frame of mind he set off for Liberty.

It was only after riding along for a few hours that it dawned on him that there was a reason for his disquiet.

He had become used to her company.

Lewis nursed his coffee while he sat at the end of the bar.

Although his last visit to Liberty had been short and nobody should have had a clear view of him, he had avoided looking through the doorway at the length of boardwalk where last week Emerson Greeley had died.

He'd not spoken to anyone other than the bartender, but he had nodded to the few customers in an open way to give the impression he didn't have anything to hide.

His concern that someone might remember him was receding when the bartender asked if he wanted a refill. Lewis nodded then asked the question he'd come here to resolve.

'I'm looking for Thomas Miller,' he said.

'Never heard of him,' the bartender said.

'He's young, perhaps in a hurry. He certainly left White Creek quickly.'

The bartender's eyes flickered in a way that a seasoned manhunter like Lewis recognized as a sign that he had seen Thomas.

'In trouble, is he?'

If no other customers were there, Lewis would have let the bartender string him along before he provided the money for which he was fishing. But with this conversation having encouraged several customers to gravitate towards the bar, he rubbed his fingers together to show he had money.

'Yup. So what'll it cost to tell me what you know?'

He slurped down the last of his coffee as he awaited an answer, but the bartender glanced at the nearest customer and provided a slight nod. This encouraged the man to lean on the bar beside Lewis.

Two other men stood on his other side while another loitered behind him.

'We've been paid to look out for men coming from White Creek,' the newcomer said in a low tone, 'or for men looking for Thomas Miller. You're doing both.'

Lewis caught the vibe of impending violence in the eager eyes of the men surrounding him. He turned to go, but the man who had positioned himself behind him was blocking his way.

'Why?' Lewis asked.

'Norton will explain.' The man looked over Lewis's shoulder at the bartender. 'Fetch Norton. He was in the stables.'

The bartender came out from behind the bar and

headed to the door.

'Norton!' he hollered over the batwings while beckoning to an unseen man. 'Come here. We've got a man from White Creek asking about Thomas Miller.'

Lewis reckoned this meeting would turn out badly, so he barged past the nearest two men and strode off towards the doorway at a determined pace.

'Hey,' a voice demanded from behind him. 'You're not going nowhere.'

Lewis ignored the demand. A hand slapped down on his shoulder aiming to halt him but he threw it off and continued walking.

The bartender swung away from the door to block his way. Lewis moved to step to his side, his action making the bartender move that way too but it was only a feint and he went the other way, brushing past his shoulder.

He'd got to within two paces of the door and he was hoping he'd get outside before he would have to run for his life, when a burly man paced up to the door.

'Norton,' someone said. 'Stop him!'

Lewis thrust his head down and pushed through the batwings, hoping to get as far as he could before anyone could waylay him, but beyond the doorway, Norton spread his arms, slapping him in the chest and halting him.

'You're staying,' he said, as men closed in on Lewis from all sides.

'I don't want no trouble,' Lewis said. 'I'm leaving.'

'The only thing you're doing is answering some questions.' Norton moved round and stood before him as the men from the saloon spilled out through the door, blocking off his exits.

Lewis shrugged and put on his most reasonable voice.

'When I said I didn't want no trouble, I meant for you. Now let me leave while you still can.'

Norton snorted a laugh, bemused by Lewis's truculence when faced by such overwhelming odds. He darted a glance at someone behind Lewis to share in his amusement.

Lewis took that as his best opportunity and thundered a blow into Norton's guts that had him folding over and gasping in pain. Then he slapped both hands on his back and threw him into the path of the men moving through the door.

Men went tumbling but he didn't wait to see how many fell as he broke into a run. He'd left his horse by the stables, as he'd done on his last brief visit, and he aimed to cover those thirty yards as quickly as possible.

He pounded across the ground, hearing the men behind him grumbling then getting up and following him. He put them from his mind and ran, but when he made to leap up on to his horse a hand slapped down on his shoulder from behind.

He tried to throw the hand off, but it gripped tightly so in a deft motion he drew his gun and swung the weapon round to slap it up under his assailant's chin.

'Get your hands off me,' he grunted, 'or I'll. . . .'

More threatening words were on his lips, but they fled from his mind unsaid.

His assailant was Cameron, his brother.

'Or you'll do what?' Cameron said with mock pleasantry.

Lewis returned a brief smile then lowered his gun. He turned to see the men from the saloon had stopped in the middle of the road. Norton was at the front and was eyeing this encounter with interest.

'I'll have to save your hide, brother.'

Cameron snorted. 'You're wrong, brother. Against our better judgement we've decided we'll be the ones who'll save your hide.'

Lewis was minded to pour scorn on Cameron's offer of help, but Norton was urging the men in the road to move closer. They took one step, then another, but then Norton signified that they should halt. Everyone turned their gaze and looked to the side.

Lewis looked too and saw Marshal Ingersoll walking around the side of the stables with Harlan trailing along behind.

Ingersoll stopped, shrugged his jacket to ensure the townsfolk saw his star, then spoke up.

'I'm Marshal Samuel Ingersoll from White Creek,' he said in a clear voice. 'No matter what your problem with this man is, you'll oblige me by answering a question. Has anyone seen Thomas Miller?'

The question made Lewis wince as Norton uttered a surly oath.

'You may have tried to save me,' Lewis said, leaning towards Cameron, 'But that question's just ruined your good work.'

With that comment he turned his back on Cameron and leapt up on to his horse.

'Why?' Cameron murmured.

'No time to answer,' Lewis said, as Norton gestured and the townsfolk moved purposefully towards them. 'Just get the hell out of here while you still can.'

Cameron watched the people advance and spread out, each man flexing his fists. Then he turned on his heel and hurried towards Ingersoll, pointing to his horse.

Harlan didn't need a second warning, but Ingersoll stayed, looking as if he'd try to reason with the men, but when they continued to advance he joined them in taking flight.

Being the only one mounted, Lewis swung his horse round and headed straight at Norton. For his part Norton stood defiantly before him, but Lewis rode on giving him no choice but to dive out of his way or be trampled.

For several strides it looked as if he'd face down the speeding mount, but at the last moment he dived aside and Lewis found himself in the midst of the crowd.

Hands grabbed for his legs seeking to dislodge him, forcing him to slap and kick them away. One man lunged for the reins but he kicked him to the ground. Two men stood before him forcing him to barge his horse into them and send them tumbling, making his horse skitter over them to reach clear space before the saloon.

By now Cameron and the others had mounted their horses and were watching the altercation with mounting horror.

He was gesturing to them to move on out when behind him someone fired a rifle, the sound echoing in the road and creating a sudden silence. Lewis looked round to see who had fired while scrambling for his own gun.

The bartender was standing outside the saloon with his rifle thrust high; he eyed Lewis with steady menace.

'That one was to the heavens,' he shouted. 'The next one sends you there.'

The bartender hefted the rifle in his hand, his change in stance letting Lewis know he was preparing to swing the rifle down and fire.

Lewis turned his gun in his grip and blasted him through the chest, hurtling him backwards into the saloon wall. Then he urged his horse across the road, not waiting for the retaliation to come.

He reached his mounted brothers and Ingersoll beside the stables and shot them a glance.

'Get out of town!' he hollered. 'You won't get

nothing here but death.'

Gunfire sounded behind him and he returned a couple of wild shots over his shoulder before his brothers accepted he was right. They drew their guns and fired at the gathered men, but they fired over their heads, giving the men enough time to scurry into hiding.

'We're not making this into a bloodbath,' Ingersoll said.

Lewis moved his horse on to join them, then turned round to survey the scene. The body of the bartender lay on the boardwalk and the other men had taken cover either in the saloon or beside the building.

'You made a big mistake when you shot him,' Norton shouted from an alley.

'We never wanted no trouble,' Ingersoll shouted. 'So this ends here if you're prepared to hear us out.'

Cameron and Harlan murmured that they agreed with this sentiment while Lewis snorted, not reckoning this plea would work. Sure enough, when they got their answer it came in the form of hot lead.

Slugs whined overhead or kicked splinters from the side of the stables.

'I told you,' Lewis said when the first volley had ended. 'They won't listen to reason.'

He fired off a speculative volley at the saloon then swung his horse around to the edge of town, but he still dallied as he waited for his brothers to join him.

Harlan and Cameron looked at Ingersoll, who

shot one last glance at the saloon, but as several men edged out to fire at them, he made his decision.

'Move on out!' he hollered with an overhead gesture.

As gunfire tore out, ripping into the ground around their horses' hoofs or whistling by their bodies, none of them needed a second order and they all swung round and galloped out of town.

Gunfire hurried them on their way, all thankfully wild, letting the four men ride past the outlying buildings unscathed.

'Looks like we got away,' Harlan shouted when they were another two hundred yards on.

Lewis looked back to see that the townsfolk had stopped firing at them, but that was only so that they could hurry to their horses to begin their pursuit.

'Nope,' he said. 'It looks like our problems are only just starting.'

CHAPTER 8

'I reckon we've thrown them off,' Lewis said.

'Don't look so pleased,' Cameron muttered. 'It's your fault they were chasing after us in the first place.'

Lewis left Ingersoll on lookout and faced Cameron.

'I got us out of there, so quit complaining.'

'But *we* weren't in no danger. We rode into town to ask if anyone had seen Thomas Miller and found you running for your life.'

'And now,' Harlan grumbled, 'they think we're with you so we're in the same trouble as you are. And we'll never find out if Thomas passed through Liberty.'

The two brothers glared at Lewis with their hands on their hips. Lewis didn't reply immediately, wondering if he should waste his time answering their complaints when they clearly didn't want to hear his explanation of what had happened.

The last few hours had been fraught.

After they'd fled the town, the seven men who had followed them had been dogged in their pursuit.

After an hour they had searched for somewhere to hole up. They had passed close to Randall's End and Lewis had remembered a place he'd seen on his previous visit. So he'd directed them to a gully that had steep sides and an entrance that was so thin it wasn't visible from the plains unless you paid careful attention.

The gully had boulder-strewn gashes on either side to hide in and they had chosen a barely accessible one high on the left hand side, holing up about twenty feet from the top. This position let them see the plains and Lewis had hoped he would be able to see their pursuers ride on by.

This relative safety hadn't cheered his brothers.

'Have you two finished?' Lewis asked. He received snarled grunts that suggested they could carry on complaining until sundown. Lewis sighed. 'If it'll calm you down, I asked about Thomas in the saloon, but mentioning him got everyone trigger-happy.'

'So you reckon he paid them to attack us?' Cameron asked.

'That's my guess.'

'Or maybe,' Harlan muttered, 'they hated your company as much as we do.'

'You won't have to suffer that for long. When we've thrown Norton's men off, I'll leave.' Lewis looked

87

around the gully, wondering which route would be the easiest to traverse. 'In fact I'll take my chances now.'

Lewis moved to climb up the twenty feet of sharply angled rock aiming to reach the top of the gully and see if he could lead his horse out that way. But Cameron moved to the side and stood in his way.

'You're not going nowhere until you tell us why you decided to go after Thomas.'

'Would you believe me if I said I'm all cut up about Jesse?'

'Nope.'

'Then I won't bother answering.'

Lewis moved to head off, but this time Ingersoll raised a hand, halting him.

'You'll answer his question and then you'll stay with us so I can make sure you don't shoot up any more towns.'

'Hey,' Harlan muttered before Lewis could reply. 'I don't want him riding with us.'

Cameron grunted the same sentiment making Ingersoll look skyward, sighing. Ingersoll moved away from keeping lookout to face them. He looked at each man in turn, shaking his head.

'The Coltaines!' he snorted. 'Why did I bring you along? Keep you apart and we get a whole town on our tail. Keep you together and you argue like you're still squabbling children.'

Lewis kicked at the ground, feeling suitably chastised. Cameron cast him a shame-faced look and the matter might have ended there, but Harlan snorted with irritation.

'The only reason we're arguing is because Lewis won't tell us why he's here. But I reckon I know why. It's because he knows more about Jesse's death than he's let on.'

'Be quiet!' Lewis snapped, his anger at his brother's attitude making his blood surge.

'I won't,' Harlan said, smirking at Lewis's reaction. 'You don't care about Jesse, so maybe you're feeling guilty. Do you know Mason Crockett? Did you—?'

'I said,' Lewis roared stepping up to Harlan, his voice echoing in the gully, 'be quiet.'

'I won't be quiet until I get an answer.'

Harlan glanced over Lewis's shoulder looking for support from Cameron and Ingersoll, but Lewis took advantage of him being distracted to launch a swinging uppercut to Harlan's chin that cracked his head back so swiftly his feet left the ground.

Harlan crashed to the ground on his back where he lay rubbing his jaw and shaking his head. But when he looked up, he was smiling.

'I'd hoped you'd do that,' he said. Slowly he got to his feet, his fists bunching. 'Now nobody will stop me teaching you the lesson I should have given you a long time ago.'

Lewis rolled his shoulders then paced towards Harlan with his hands held out ready to grab him if he made a move in either direction. In response Harlan backed away towards the sheer slope behind him while beckoning him on and looking Lewis up and down as he awaited an opening.

Harlan stopped two paces from the edge, glanced backwards to check his position, then, while apparently off guard, he kicked off and ran at Lewis. His sudden movement surprised Lewis and he didn't have time to move out of the way.

With a leading shoulder Harlan slammed into Lewis's chest and carried him back for several paces before Lewis could dig in a heel and stop himself. Then he slapped both hands on Harlan's shoulders and twisted, trying to wrestle him to the ground. But Harlan wrapped his arms around Lewis's midriff and, gripping tightly, tried to shove Lewis in the opposite direction.

They strained, neither man getting the upper hand until Lewis moved a foot to get better traction and his heel turned on a stone, jerking him to the side. Harlan used the motion to twist him and they both went down. Lewis landed on his back with Harlan on top of him.

He looked up into Harlan's eyes and saw the pent up anger burning there that could be extinguished only by violence.

Harlan raised himself slightly, his right hand coming free. Then he punched Lewis in the stomach.

The blow landed without much force, so Harlan drew back his arm even further, but the blow didn't land, as Lewis pushed a palm up under Harlan's chin. The force from his straightening arm went into a teeth-rattling blow that jerked Harlan's head back and made him fall away.

Lewis followed through by shoving and kicking him off. Then he scrambled to his feet and stood over Harlan, waiting for him to get up.

Harlan glared up at him while feeling his jaw and catching his breath. He rolled his shoulders then slowly got to his feet, his eyes taking in Lewis's posture as he planned his next assault.

'That's enough, Harlan,' Cameron urged.

'Don't stop him,' Lewis said pleasantly. 'Your brother's been spoiling for a fight since the moment he saw me. Now is the right time to teach him he's not got what it takes to take on men like me.'

The taunt made Harlan snort his breath and advance a determined pace on Lewis, who saw in his eyes a burning hatred that said this time he aimed to engage in more than a mere tussle. So Lewis cautiously backed away.

'You two are stopping this fight,' Cameron snapped. 'Right now.'

A retort came to Lewis's lips, but then a footfall sounded behind him. Somebody cocked a gun.

Lewis was about to confront Cameron, assuming he was strengthening his ultimatum. But then the senses that had kept him alive through numerous scrapes told him he'd been mistaken.

He dropped to one knee while swirling round at the hip, his gun coming to hand. With a single shot he picked out the man coming over the top of the ridge, his gun cocked and aimed at them. The blast hit the man's shoulder and sent him flying backwards to land out of view.

'What the—?' Harlan murmured.

'Get down!' Lewis snapped. 'You were making too much noise. They've found us.'

'You were making the noise,' Harlan whined, but he had the sense to stop arguing; he headed towards the nearest mound and hunkered down.

Ingersoll and Cameron joined him while Lewis stayed put, preferring to keep in sight all the possible places where their pursuers might spring up.

He'd been waiting for a minute when movement caught his eye to his left; a man was bobbing up to look over the ridge. Lewis started to swing his gun towards him, but at that moment three other men jerked up to that man's right.

Lewis blasted the nearest man in the chest, sending him reeling, then swung his gun towards the others. He got the first one in his sights but by then they had all turned their guns on him.

He dived to his side and lay on his chest, the action saving him from a burst of gunfire that tore into the ground where he'd been kneeling. He rolled twice. Then, with his hands thrust out and his body presenting a small profile, he aimed again at the left hand man.

He fired. His slug caught him high in the chest, but the other two men had followed his progress and

92

still had their guns trained on Lewis.

Gunfire roared, but Lewis was relieved to see the two men go sprawling as Ingersoll's rapid gunfire blasted into them.

The man he'd shot flopped down to lie with his arms dangling over the edge of the gully and the other two came tumbling down and lay in a cloud of dust between Lewis and Ingersoll. Both men then were still and even without checking Lewis presumed they'd get no more trouble from them.

Lewis nodded to Ingersoll. 'Obliged.'

'We both did well,' Ingersoll said. 'We get 'em all?'

Lewis thought back. 'Seven came after us and we can see three bodies. You check down the gully, I'll check over the top.'

Ingersoll nodded, but Cameron raised a hand.

'What about us?' he asked.

Lewis glanced at Cameron and Harlan. He couldn't help but smile on seeing that they were licking their lips while nervously looking around, the brief shootout having removed their previous truculence.

'You keep lookout.' Lewis got to his feet and clambered up to the top of the ridge.

When he peered over the top he saw another of the men they'd shot lying on his chest in a spreading pool of blood. This left three men unaccounted for, so he edged along towards the position where the first man he'd shot had fallen from sight.

Something moved to his side and he swung round

towards it. He saw that it came from two men running away down the side of the ridge towards the plains, leaping from rock to rock as they escaped.

Lewis aimed at the nearest man's back, weighing up whether or not he should shoot. At this distance he could hit him easily, but instead he made his way along the edge of the ridge.

A wounded man lying on his side came into view. Closer to, he saw that it was Norton, the ringleader of the enraged townsfolk back in Liberty. He was on the edge of a steep slope, his and the other dead men's horses waiting some two hundred feet below. He was clutching his shoulder and groaning in pain.

Lewis jumped down to land beside him, then kicked his gun away and sent it rolling down the slope. Norton looked up at him through pained eyes.

'You were on the lookout for men from White Creek who were following Thomas Miller,' Lewis said. 'Why?'

'Got nothing to say to you,' Norton muttered.

Lewis hunkered down beside him. With the barrel of his gun he poked Norton's wounded shoulder, making him flinch. As long moments passed and Lewis said nothing else, sweat broke out on the man's brow.

'Many men have said they wouldn't answer my questions,' Lewis said finally, speaking slowly. He pushed Norton over to lie him on his back then dragged him closer to the edge of the ridge. He glanced down at the long drop to the ground below. Then he looked at Norton and smiled. 'They were all wrong.'

CHAPTER 9

Fifteen minutes after he'd left to scout around Lewis returned to his brothers and Ingersoll.

'We get 'em all?' Ingersoll asked.

'Nope,' Lewis said. 'The rest are over there, but they won't cause us no trouble. One man's dead and two men are hightailing it away. The other man was Norton, the ringleader, but he's wounded and he's slunk off to lick his wounds. I suggest we take the chance to leave.'

Ingersoll nodded, but his brothers looked at each other then shook their heads.

'We're not leaving with you,' Harlan said. 'We'll find our brother's killer on our own.'

'I wasn't offering. I meant it's time for us to get away. I know where I'm going. You can go wherever you want.'

Lewis moved to leave, but Ingersoll coughed, making him turn back.

'You can go,' Ingersoll said, 'but only after you've told us how you worked out where Thomas had gone.'

Lewis considered the steely-eyed lawman, then sighed.

'I assume you followed his tracks.' Lewis waited until Ingersoll nodded. 'Well, I've hunted men before. Liberty is the main town west of White Creek, so that's where I reckoned he'd go. I was right.'

'And your next hunch?'

Earlier, with time pressing as Norton had pleaded for his life, he had provided one crucial piece of information in the hope that it'd satisfy him.

'Thomas turned south.' Lewis pointed.

Ingersoll narrowed his eyes. 'How do you know that?'

'I don't. It's another hunch. Follow me if you like it, or go another way if you don't.' Lewis looked at his brothers and shrugged. 'It don't matter none to me.'

Lewis considered the trail ahead, noting that a quarter mile ahead someone had stopped and was watching them approach. Lewis couldn't tell if this person represented trouble but he looked back at Ingersoll to check he'd noticed the rider.

Ingersoll nodded, but his brothers ignored him as usual.

Since leaving the gully they had tracked Thomas for three days. Norton had given him a direction and they had proved it was the right one when they'd met

97

travellers coming in the opposite direction. This group had seen a young rider pass by in a hurry.

When they next met a traveller they learnt that they were gaining on him, but they were still a day behind and remained unsure as to where his ultimate destination would be.

Initially Lewis had had a worrying idea. Fort Lord, where he'd lived after he'd left White Creek and the place where Emerson Greeley had killed his wife, was one hundred miles to the south.

This uncomfortable thought receded when Thomas's route veered him towards Parker's Gulch. But as he'd passed through this town four months ago in his search for Emerson Greeley, he stayed apprehensive.

Worse, it ensured he couldn't shake off the thought that Thomas's visit to Liberty would connect to Emerson Greeley's final taunt, even if he couldn't see how.

Throughout their journey they had maintained a vigilant lookout for reprisals from Norton's surviving men. Even though they had seen no sign of anyone following them, his companions matched his pensive mood and rarely engaged him in conversation. . . .

With a flinch, Lewis realized he'd been brooding and he had ridden to within a hundred yards of the person on the trail. At the same time he registered that the others were talking about this forthcoming encounter.

'Never expected to see her again,' Cameron said.

'What's she doing out here?' Harlan said.

'Don't know. If you want the answer, ask her or ask Lewis.'

Lewis shook himself then focused on the person ahead, resolving the form into that of a woman: Elizabeth Fisher.

His heart thudded with joy, making him smile until, with a cough, he got himself under control. Then he hurried on to meet her.

The others drew to a halt to let them speak privately, not that there was anything personal he wanted to say other than to ask the questions they had asked.

'What are you doing here?' he said when he drew his horse up.

'Now that sure is a fine welcome,' she said, placing a hand on her hip to show she was feigning irritation, 'after you haven't seen me for almost a week.'

'I never expected to see you again after you slipped away in the middle of the night.'

She smiled. 'It sounds as if you missed me.'

'I did.' Lewis waited until her eyes twinkled with delight. 'You were like an annoying boil. When it goes, you miss the irritation.'

Her jaw firmed before she dismissed the matter with a shake of the head, but when she spoke her voice was lower and perhaps hurt.

'I missed you though.'

Lewis considered his reply before he spoke, feeling guilty for having insulted her and not wishing to do it again.

'That mean you've not found anyone else to. . . .' He glanced over his shoulder to confirm the others couldn't hear him. 'To help you?'

'I haven't.' She sighed. 'And I'm not sure what I want to do now.'

'That's sensible thinking.' He edged his horse closer to her. 'So why have you sought me out again?'

'For the same reason. If I'm having second thoughts, I'd hoped you might have them too. You were hurting when I left you, twisting yourself up inside about why Liberty was on that bookmark. So I decided to help you.'

'Help?'

'I've found Thomas.' She pointed over her shoulder. 'He's stopped a few miles out of Parker's Gulch, sitting around looking worried like you are. I can take you to him.'

'And you've done this to help me, with no other motive than to put my mind at rest?'

She opened her mouth then closed it and sighed, suggesting she'd decided not to provide her original answer.

'Do you want to see Thomas or do you want to risk that he's moved on?'

'Thomas,' he said.

She nodded and moved to the side to join him. After beckoning the others and providing them with the same minimal details, she headed back down the trail. With an exchange of bemused glances, at a steady pace they headed after her towards Parker's Gulch.

Five miles out of town she veered them away to head across the plains and another five miles on she pointed out a homestead in the distance where they'd find Thomas.

Only then did Marshal Ingersoll ask the obvious question.

'How did you find him?'

'And why?' Cameron asked before she could answer.

'I asked around,' she said. 'I got lucky when some travellers had seen him heading away from Liberty. So I followed him here.'

'And yet,' Ingersoll said, 'none of the travellers we questioned mentioned seeing a woman.'

'They wouldn't. A lone woman has to be careful who sees her.'

This answer quietened Ingersoll, although the sceptical look in his eyes stayed, and Lewis couldn't blame him. He also found it hard to believe she'd found Thomas more efficiently than he had.

He put that concern from his mind when they were close enough to the homestead to see that a horse was mooching nearby. There were two buildings – a barn and a house. Both were badly burnt and lacked roofs and they appeared abandoned.

About two hundred yards away Lewis saw a man sitting on the porch. He had bowed his head to look at the ground between his feet.

'Thomas,' Cameron murmured, receiving a grunt of confirmation from the other men.

Their quarry didn't look up even when Lewis felt sure they were close enough for him to hear them approaching and so it was left to Ingersoll to holler to him.

Thomas jerked as if shot, then looked up. He glanced around, appearing as if he were looking for somewhere to hide, but then he nodded as he recognized them and with a resigned slap of his thighs he stood to meet them.

'Stay where you are, Thomas,' Ingersoll said, 'and keep those hands where I can see them.'

'I won't do anything.' Thomas twitched his head to the side while raising and lowering his eyebrows. 'And I can't help you, so you might as well go back to White Creek.'

As Thomas continued to provide odd facial expressions and twitch as if he were having a minor fit, Ingersoll led the others in dismounting and going over to him.

'You're in a lot of trouble,' he said, eyeing him with bemusement. 'But we're prepared to hear you out. So calm down and explain yourself.'

'It's too late,' Thomas murmured with a resigned sigh, although he still gave another twitch of his head.

'Why?'

Thomas didn't reply and it was left for another voice to speak up from within the shell of the house.

'Because,' that man said, as he stepped through the doorway, 'what Thomas was trying to tell you was that you're the ones who have ridden into a heap of trouble.'

Thomas gave Ingersoll a shamefaced look as a second man followed the first. Both men had guns brandished. The first roved his gun in a steady arc across the gathered people while the second jabbed his gun into the small of Thomas's back.

'What's the set-up here?' Ingersoll asked, but before either man could answer, Lewis stepped up to join him.

'I recognize these two men,' he said. 'They ran away after they ambushed us near Randall's End. Then Norton gave me directions so that I could follow Thomas. I should have realized he gave me that information too readily.'

'You should.' The man smirked. 'And now we're taking you all on a little journey.'

Thomas started to shake while gulping loudly, making Ingersoll look at him.

'What's wrong?' he asked.

Thomas tried to speak, but the words were unintelligible and emerged only as gasps of ragged breathing.

'He's trying to say,' the man holding the gun against his back said, 'that he's bait. And he knows what happens to bait when the prey arrives.'

'Please . . . please don't,' Thomas murmured.

While grinning, the man leaned forward to look

him in the eye.

'Don't panic. You did a good job. So I'll make this easy on you.'

The man tensed and realizing that he was about to shoot, Lewis lunged forward and grabbed Thomas's shoulder. He dragged him aside sending him to the porch on his chest, leaving the man standing awkwardly with his gun thrust out.

Ingersoll must also have realized that he was going to kill Thomas as he scrambled for his gun.

The man stuck out a foot to right himself and jerked his gun to the side to shoot Thomas, but then he saw that both Lewis and Ingersoll were drawing their guns. He stopped the motion and in a moment of indecision he searched both men's eyes wondering who to turn his gun on first.

Ingersoll made him pay for that indecision and blasted a low shot into his guts that made him fold in two, stagger a pace forward then keel over.

The second man moved to scramble into hiding in the house. He managed three paces before Lewis caught him with a high shot to the back that made him fall against the doorway where he held on for a moment before sliding down it and slamming to the dirt inside.

'These the only two?' Ingersoll asked the prone Thomas.

When Thomas gave a nervous nod, he went to stand over the man who had fallen through the doorway. He checked on him then provided a sorry shake of the head. Lewis checked on the second man then also shook his head.

'Their deaths,' he said, 'leave us with plenty of questions.'

'They do, but hopefully Thomas can provide the answers.'

Ingersoll joined Lewis and the rest in looking at Thomas who was now being helped to his feet by Elizabeth while Cameron and Harlan eyed him with distrust.

'I'd have come back to White Creek and told you everything,' Thomas said, his voice gaining confidence. 'You didn't need to follow me here. Although I'm pleased that you did.'

Ingersoll opened his mouth to reply, but before he could speak Harlan stepped forward.

'Did you kill Jesse?' he demanded. 'Were you up on the ridge when he died? Who's Mason Crockett?'

Faced with Harlan's irritation, Thomas opened and closed his mouth soundlessly then pointed with a shaking hand behind him.

'All the answers are out the back.'

'And what are they? Why did you run? Who were these people?'

'Enough, Harlan!' Lewis snapped. 'Stay here and start being nice to him. He's had a rough time from the look of it. I'll see what's back there.'

He didn't wait for Harlan's agreement and set off around the derelict house. Elizabeth followed on behind.

At the back of the house he saw the horses the men had used to get here, but nothing untoward. An overgrown flattened area that had probably once been used to grow vegetables was ahead.

Then fifty feet from the house he saw the two mounds and the crosses. He glanced at Elizabeth, who provided a sympathetic frown, before he set off towards the crosses.

When he stood before them he saw that both people had died three months ago. On his first reading of the details he didn't recognize either name. He tipped back his hat to scratch his forehead wondering why Thomas thought this explained everything.

He read the names again.

He gulped. His vision blurred and the ground seemed to lurch so that he had to thrust out a leg to stay upright. When the initial shock had receded he removed his hat and held it before him.

'Do you know these. . . ?' Elizabeth asked, then trailed off when she saw Lewis's grim expression.

'I do,' Lewis murmured, his voice gruff with emotion.

'Then does this end your quest?'

'No,' Lewis said. 'It starts it.'

CHAPTER 10

Lewis and Elizabeth stood before the graves considering the few words written on the crosses.

Unlike the previous time he had stood in such a position, Lewis felt tired and stiff, symptoms of a grief he hadn't expected to ever feel again.

He could tell from Elizabeth's nervous glances at him that she wanted an explanation, but he only wanted to voice it once and his brothers had to be the first to hear the words.

Presently the others came round the house and saw him standing over the graves. Thomas spoke to Ingersoll and then he and the lawman stayed back. Cameron and Harlan came forward to join him.

'Whose are they?' Cameron asked, eyeing Lewis's stern expression with consternation.

'You'd better see for yourself,' Lewis said, stepping back.

With Harlan beside him, Cameron stood before the crosses and read the first brief legend.

'Stacy Malone . . . never heard of him.'

'And the second.'

'Del . . . Delores Malone.' Cameron coughed as the obvious thought hit him. He gathered his composure with a shrug but his voice was shaking when he continued. 'And she died on the same day as Stacy did, three months ago.'

'Exactly. Stacy and Delores Malone.'

'I don't know these people,' Cameron said guardedly. 'This is a coincidence; it has to be.'

'It's not.'

Cameron gulped and read the legends again, shaking his head with the same display of disbelief Lewis had felt when he'd first seen them.

'What does he mean?' Harlan demanded, his voice high-pitched. 'Because all I see is the graves of two people who have the same Christian names as Thomas Miller's brother who died twelve years ago and our sister who ran away from home.'

'Twelve years ago,' Cameron said.

'But it don't make no sense,' he bleated, his voice breaking as he struggled to keep himself from accepting that this terrible discovery was in fact the truth. 'And how did Thomas find these people? And what's this got to do with Jesse's murder?'

Both men looked at Lewis and he offered a consoling frown.

'That is our sister lying there,' he said. 'And her husband is lying beside her. That's all I know for sure. The rest is a guess.'

'Which is?' Cameron asked.

Lewis didn't reply immediately, giving himself time to put his thoughts in order before uttering his carefully chosen words.

'Twelve years ago Jesse said he killed Stacy Miller, except he didn't. Stacy came here and Delores joined him. They lived a contented life until—'

'You're wrong!' Harlan screeched. 'Stacy's dead back in White Creek. The Millers buried him.'

'And somebody dug up his grave,' Cameron murmured, 'a few months before these people died.'

Harlan gulped, the slow dawning realization that had come to Lewis and then Cameron making him lower his head.

'Then who,' he murmured, 'was buried in Stacy Miller's grave?'

Lewis looked to the house where Ingersoll was escorting Thomas towards them.

'We all know the answer to that, but Thomas should be the one who says it.'

When Thomas joined them he looked at each of them in turn, his face set in a deep frown that conveyed both fear of what they might do and sympathy for what they'd seen.

'It was Mason Crockett,' he said. 'Twelve years ago Jesse accidentally killed the wrong man. He covered up what he'd done and claimed the body was my brother's, but now Mason's son, Norton—'

'Norton!' Cameron muttered as the others glanced at each other, everyone gathering the

109

significance of the name. 'He was waiting for us in Liberty.'

'I know that now. He's been getting revenge on everyone responsible. He started with Stacy and your sister, then moved on to Jesse.'

'And I had him,' Lewis said, 'lying wounded at the end of my gun, but I let him live.'

'You weren't to know,' Thomas said. 'The men who were holding me worked for him as do a whole lot more.'

Everyone stood in stunned silence for a minute before Cameron patted Thomas's back.

'This is terrible,' he said then pointed at the graves. 'But at least these two proved that the Miller family and the Coltaine family can get on together, so you have nothing to fear from us.'

Thomas breathed a sigh of relief, but he still backed away for a pace.

'Before you say things like that, you need to know that if it hadn't been for me, these two would have gone on proving our families can get on.'

'You're not to blame.'

'I am. I wanted to know the full story behind what happened to Stacy. I asked around and found people in Redemption who'd seen things. Then I found Norton.' Thomas lowered his head. 'For twelve years he'd been searching for the reason why his father had disappeared. What I told him filled in the missing pieces and led to this.'

Cameron looked at Harlan who had bowed his

head, his normal argumentative attitude showing no sign of surfacing, before he replied.

'We forgive you,' he said. 'All that matters now is that these deaths turn out to be the last.'

Harlan nodded. 'Our families could be in danger with nobody to protect them and we're more than a week away from home. We need to get back.'

'We do,' Cameron said as Harlan looked to the house, appearing as if he'd head to his horse and gallop off immediately. 'But it'll be sundown in an hour. We'll rest up here for the night then leave at first light.'

Harlan rocked from foot to foot, looking as if he was about to argue, but then nodded.

With nothing else to discuss, Cameron set off for the abandoned house with Harlan. Thomas and Ingersoll filed in behind, while Lewis stayed back to cast a last look at his sister's grave.

Elizabeth joined him and offered a supportive smile.

'That was a hard thing for you to find,' she said. 'What will you do now?'

'Whether Norton killed my wife or just my sister and brother, I'll kill him,' he said in a matter-of-fact manner, then coughed. 'But I guess finding Delores saves me from making that other journey I was planning to make.'

'What journey was. . . ?' She narrowed her eyes then nodded. 'So your sister was the woman you'd planned to search for?'

Lewis nodded while looking at her from the corner of his eye. He noted that she was pursing her lips to avoid smiling.

Despite the situation, that warmed him.

The campfire they'd lit in the corner of the derelict house cast flickering light across everyone's faces. The sheltered spot made them warmer than they'd been on any previous night of their journey, but nobody was talking.

Lewis hadn't had a chance to speak to Thomas yet as he'd not moved away from the group. He didn't want to speak with him openly and draw attention to his problem, but he didn't know how much longer he could cope with not knowing if Emerson Greeley fitted into Norton's vengeance spree.

He'd withdrawn to the back of the house away from the others to write up his journal, but the words hadn't come because he couldn't get his thoughts in order.

It was possible that Emerson had been hired to kill *him* but then his wife had got in the way. Yet no matter how he looked at it, the dead people either had been responsible for Mason's demise or had kept it secret. As he hadn't been involved, there was no reason other than the family connection for him to have hired Emerson in the first place.

When Elizabeth returned from cleaning their plates she sat with him. For the last few hours everyone had stayed away from them to give them

112

space and curiously this hadn't irritated him.

He moved aside to give her room to sit and in return she rewarded him with a beaming smile.

'You seem calmer,' she said.

He snorted. 'Nope.'

'Any clearer as to what happened?'

'Nope.'

'And there was me thinking you might be talkative now.' She looked aloft, sighing. 'But if you won't talk to me, talk to them. They'll understand.'

'They might.' Lewis sighed. 'But I can't talk when I haven't sorted out my problems. Four months ago I passed through Parker's Gulch while looking for Emerson. Delores was still alive then but I didn't know that. Maybe he was looking for her. Maybe if I'd found him sooner she'd have still been alive. Maybe—'

Elizabeth leaned towards him and lowered her voice to ensure the others by the fire wouldn't hear.

'Don't do this to yourself. Believe me, I understand the torment. I've thought of nothing else but making my husband's killer suffer. I want him to care for someone as I did, then before he dies to experience the pain of knowing he'll never see that person again. But what you said last week made sense. Vengeance doesn't keep you warm at night, so perhaps I shouldn't seek revenge.'

'That is the best for you.'

'Then why can't it be the best for you?'

'Because I don't know the full story. I can't think

113

of anything else when I don't know.'

'I understand.' She took a deep breath then raised herself and called out to the group by the fire. 'Thomas, why did you go to Liberty and not straight here?'

Lewis shot her a glare, but she leaned forward to avoid catching his eye.

'It's a long story,' Thomas said. He looked around and saw that everyone was looking at him with tired and brooding eyes. 'And I don't reckon anyone's in the mood to hear it right now.'

'Maybe not, but the short version might help.'

Thomas received brief nods from Cameron and Harlan. Lewis gripped his hands tightly to avoid showing a reaction.

Thomas took a deep breath. 'Norton had heard about the men who had been searching for Stacy twelve years ago.'

'Men?' Lewis snapped, the realization of what he'd said making him interrupt the story.

'Some of the details he had were wrong. Although I guess we'll never know the full truth now, the story we pieced together was that Stacy had tried to put Jesse off his trail by selling his horse to Mason Crockett. Jesse followed the horse and when Mason went through a pass at night he ambushed and killed him before he realized his mistake.'

'A sorry tale,' Cameron said.

Thomas murmured that he agreed then continued talking, but Lewis didn't listen.

Elizabeth was looking at him, also shocked at hearing that Norton reckoned more than one man had been involved in his father's death. Worse, Mason had been killed in the same way as Lewis had accidentally killed Raymond Templeton.

Lewis placed his hands over his ears willing himself to think this through, but no matter how he looked at it, Thomas's tale was too bizarre to be a coincidence.

'And Liberty?' he barked, creating sudden silence as it had interrupted whatever Thomas had been saying. 'How does that tie in with you going to Liberty?'

Harlan murmured about Lewis's rudeness before Thomas replied.

'The first time I met Norton, a man was with him and they were talking openly about what that man did. He—'

'Who was he?'

'Emerson Greeley. Like Norton he'd come from Liberty. When I heard that he'd been—'

'I've heard enough,' Lewis said.

He stood and left the house. He didn't think about where he was going and he didn't know how long he wandered but when he stopped his broody pacing he was standing before his sister's grave.

He considered the legend on her cross, wondering what sort of person she had become, and searched for a memory of her back in White Ridge.

Just like with his wife, no recollection would come,

115

so he shook himself then hunkered down to idly pull out a few tangled weeds from the mound.

A shadow cast by the fire played across the grave and he looked up to see that Elizabeth had followed him, but she stayed some distance away and merely watched him with her head cocked to one side. After a few minutes he joined her.

'Has that helped to clarify all this?' she asked.

'Yeah. . . .' He sighed. 'The endless trail of vengeance continues.'

'It doesn't have to be endless,' she whispered, her voice cracking with suppressed emotion. 'You can end the trail here and let the law deal with Norton.'

'Why should I do that?'

She looked at him with her eyebrows raised as if he should know the answer. Then she threw herself forward and planted a firm kiss on his lips.

He was so surprised he drew away but that only made her press herself against him more firmly. So he pushed her away, the feeling overcoming him that the last woman who had been that intimate with him had been his wife, just hours before he'd found her dead body.

That made her eyes flare with anger and she lunged forward and slapped his cheek.

They stared at each other, her through watering eyes and he with his cheek stinging, and then they were on each other, pressing, holding, feeling. . . .

It was some time later before either of them spoke and she asked the obvious question, although the coyness of her tone surprised him.

'Has that helped you to decide what you'll do next?'

'It has,' he said.

CHAPTER 11

Cameron was the first to wake. The others rose quickly, each man eager to start the return journey to White Creek. While Ingersoll put out the fire Thomas and Harlan joined him in heading to their horses.

'We'll have to come here again some time,' Cameron said.

'It would be good for us all to do that,' Thomas said.

Cameron noted his emphasis. 'You're right. Proof that our two families can get along would help everyone move on.'

'I doubt it'll help the Millers after all these years,' Harlan grumbled, then shot an ashamed look at Thomas. 'Not that any of us have a problem with you.'

'And not,' Thomas said, 'that any of us have a problem with you.'

As Lewis and Elizabeth hadn't returned to the fire

the previous night Cameron veered away to ensure they were ready to leave. He coughed several times and made plenty of noise before he headed towards the mound of rocks where they'd taken up residence. But he saw that Elizabeth was already awake, sitting on the rocks and looking at the lightening horizon.

'We're heading back to White Ridge,' he said.

She didn't reply and so he had to repeat his comment before she stood and headed over to him.

'I'm not,' she said. 'Lewis has gone, and I'm going after him.'

Cameron sighed, feeling in two minds. He was pleased that his brother's departure stopped him from having to suffer the constant disagreements. But the fact that Lewis had been right about Jesse's past mistake being responsible for what was happening now meant that he had started to appreciate his viewpoint.

'Then I wish you luck,' Cameron said.

She frowned. 'But there's more. You heard what Thomas said last night. Norton reckons more than one person killed his father.'

Cameron nodded, now seeing what was distressing her the most.

'Norton thinks Lewis was involved too because he originally rode off with Jesse, so Lewis has gone after Norton?'

She nodded and, in guilty embarrassment because he hadn't thought about the danger Lewis might be in, Cameron beckoned the others to join them. He explained the situation and Harlan provided the answer he'd expected.

'That's good news,' he declared. 'It means we won't have to put up with him no longer.'

Harlan's contemptuous attitude helped to put Cameron's thoughts in order.

'That don't go for me. I'm going with Elizabeth to find Lewis before he finds Norton.'

'Why?' Harlan spluttered.

'Because despite everything, he's my brother and he's sorting out a family problem.'

'But ... but. . . .' Harlan murmured, waving his arms as he struggled to voice his opinion on just how bad an idea this was, letting Ingersoll speak.

'And I'll come with you,' he said. 'If Lewis reckons he can find Norton, I need to be there.'

'But,' Harlan snapped, finally finding his voice, 'we can't risk our families. We don't know for sure that he can find Norton. While we're standing around here talking, Norton might already be in White Creek planning to attack our home.'

'You're right, and for that reason you should go back with Thomas.'

'I'm not going back there either,' Thomas said. 'I started this when I found Norton, so I'll stay with you.'

Harlan considered everyone, and they all looked at him with firm expressions that said they wouldn't change their minds. So with a muttered oath he slapped his thigh in exasperation.

'All right,' he said, 'if you're all going to act like damn fools, I might as well do so too.'

While they tracked east then south, Elizabeth remained as quiet as Lewis had been, providing no details on how she knew where he'd go.

Cameron had expected that she would direct them back towards Liberty, but when she didn't his scepticism that she had taken the right route grew. But he relaxed when, in the afternoon, Marshal Ingersoll used his uncanny ability to find people in the most deserted of places to confirm that a lone rider had been seen three hours earlier.

Despite adopting a mile-eating pace they had yet to catch sight of him, but late on the second day after leaving Parker's Gulch Elizabeth told them their destination.

'It's near Fort Lord,' she said, 'at a homestead about ten miles out of town, but I don't know where exactly.'

'And how do you know this?' Cameron asked.

Elizabeth didn't answer immediately, her darting eyes suggesting she was considering her response carefully.

'The men who held Thomas said they planned to take us somewhere. This is the place.'

Cameron looked at Ingersoll and saw the scepticism in his eyes, but when Ingersoll picked up a trail they accepted her word for now.

121

He led them across an area of scrub until a homestead appeared ahead. Disturbingly, it was similar to the one they'd left behind, consisting of two abandoned buildings, both fire damaged.

This made everyone murmur uncomfortably about the coincidence, this murmuring only ending when Cameron pointed out that a horse was tethered beside the derelict barn. The walls of both buildings were only a few feet high but he couldn't see Lewis in either.

Ingersoll moved to check out the house but before he reached it Elizabeth dismounted and hurried to the barn. She glanced over the short wall, put a hand to her chest, then sighed with relief.

She said something. When she appeared to get an answer she smiled then swung her legs over the wall and ducked down, disappearing from sight. The men gave her several minutes to emerge, but when she didn't, they decided that Cameron should approach the barn first.

He followed the route she'd taken then peered over the wall and saw that she was sitting with Lewis. They both had their backs against the wall and were silent.

'So,' Cameron said when Lewis glanced up at him, 'as we've spent the last two days finding you, I reckon you should pay us the courtesy of explaining what you're doing here.'

'I don't have to answer to you,' Lewis said, looking straight ahead, 'and I never asked you to follow me.

122

Go back to White Creek and look after your families.'

'As we reckon you're after Norton, we're staying to help you. Wherever you go, we'll go too.'

'And what good will that do?' Lewis snorted a harsh laugh. 'I saw you and Harlan cowering in that gully when Norton's men attacked us. You both think you're tough but I had to save your hides. I'm not doing that again. So run along and keep yourselves safe.'

Cameron bit his lip, trying to avoid Lewis riling him into having another pointless argument. Harlan, though, had no such qualms. He hurried over to join them then clambered over the wall to face Lewis.

'We're not listening to your demands and as we've seen no sign of Norton Crockett, tell us why you reckon you can find him. If we like your reasoning, we'll stay with you. If not, we'll leave.'

'I'm not saying nothing,' Lewis murmured. 'So go away.'

'I'm staying until I get an answer, one way or the other.' Harlan glanced at his fist. 'We got interrupted back outside Liberty, but we can finish what we started now.'

'I'm not fighting with you in this barn of all places,' Lewis murmured, his voice sounding tired.

'Why not?' Harlan demanded.

Lewis merely looked at Harlan, sneered then rolled round to kneel. He looked over the top of the short wall and ran his gaze along the horizon.

Harlan rocked back and forth on his heels, but

with Lewis ignoring him, said nothing else beyond muttering to himself. Cameron moved to the side to stand in his eye line. He still didn't get a reaction and after a minute of waiting he climbed over the wall to join Harlan.

'You can't ignore us for ever, Lewis,' he said, facing his back. 'And you'll never make me believe that you want us to go because you care about what might happen to us. You don't care about anyone. You still don't care about Jesse, and you even abandoned Elizabeth.'

Lewis snorted his breath through his nostrils then slowly stood. For several seconds he stared at the horizon then swung round to face them.

'You're right. I don't care about anyone right now, but that don't mean I'm not capable of doing so.'

Lewis glanced at Elizabeth, but her only reaction was a slow nod.

While Harlan muttered that he didn't believe him, Cameron sneered and took a pace closer. His movement made Lewis grip his hands tightly then lower his head to look at Cameron's boots.

'You're not capable of caring,' Cameron shouted, waving his arms as the anger that had festered in his mind for the last two weeks overcame him. 'You're Lewis, a man who doesn't care about anyone but himself; a man who ran away from us; a man who ran away from the first decent woman he'd met. You're a worthless varmint, Lewis, who causes trouble wherever he goes and who I hate for a whole heap of reasons, the biggest being that you soil the good Coltaine name.'

Cameron had wanted to say something like that after Lewis had been unmoved by Jesse's death, but his words didn't appear to concern Lewis. Only the fact he was standing close to him appeared to interest him as he continued to stare at his boots.

'I'll tell you this only once,' he said with steady menace, 'you'll move away from that spot or brother or no brother I'll tear you apart with my bare hands.'

Cameron viewed that comment as at least a sign that he was getting through to him and so mockingly he kicked dirt from side to side.

'I like standing here, so why should I move, you worthless heap of trash?'

'Because,' Lewis said, looking up and transfixing Cameron with his stern gaze, 'this building used to be my barn and that's the spot where six months ago I found my wife's body.'

Elizabeth shrieked then put her hand to her mouth, although Cameron reckoned from the way she then stood quickly and placed a hand on Lewis's shoulder that this wasn't news to her.

For his part Cameron placed his raised foot to the ground, feeling giddy, ashamed, embarrassed. He moved aside, an apology on his lips, but he decided it would sound too trite after the enormity of the insult he'd just uttered.

'You were married?' he said.

'A year after I left White Creek I settled down,'

Lewis said, his voice gruff. 'I built this home. Then it all got taken away.'

'Norton Crockett?'

'Yup.' Lewis shrugged. 'He hired someone to do it, but no matter, he was behind it. So you and Harlan ride off home and make sure the same thing doesn't happen to your families. Or you'll turn out like me, not caring about anyone but yourself, a worthless varmint who causes trouble wherever he goes and who soils the good Coltaine name.'

Cameron reckoned he deserved that sarcasm. As he struggled for the right words to say it was left for Harlan to convey his thoughts.

'We're not leaving you until we get Norton Crockett,' he said in a matter-of-fact manner.

Cameron nodded. 'I agree. We get him together.'

'I can't stop you,' Lewis said.

Cameron wondered if he should apologize, but on considering the unexpected common purpose his outburst had instilled in them, he reckoned it had done everyone some good.

'How do we find him?' he asked instead.

'We don't. He'll come here.'

'How can you be so sure that this is the place those men planned to take us?'

'Because Norton has always been one step ahead of us.'

He walked off to the corner of the barn. There, burnt wood was piled in a heap.

Lewis gestured at it and Cameron moved a large

plank aside to reveal a mouldering coffin. Rents in the sides displayed rags and yellowed bones.

'The infamous Mason Crockett?' he asked.

'It has to be. And that means Norton is out there somewhere.'

Cameron let the plank drop to cover the body of the man his brother had killed in error twelve years ago.

'Then we wait,' he said.

CHAPTER 12

By sundown the group had organized themselves.

They had paired up: Lewis and Elizabeth stayed together in the barn. Harlan and Cameron took the main building and Thomas and Ingersoll situated themselves away from the buildings on a mound that would let them see anyone approaching.

Each couple took turns to sleep, but the night passed without incident leaving the arrival of first light as the time when for the first time, Lewis questioned himself.

'Why are you so sure Norton will come?' Elizabeth asked, matching his thoughts. 'He might have just dumped that body here.'

'Norton killed in revenge for his father's murder. I don't think he'd just leave the body. He'll come.'

'When?'

'That's his decision. We have to be ready.' He pointed at the terrain, taking in the lightening horizons visible all around and blocked only by the

128

mound where Thomas and Ingersoll were hiding. 'And this is an excellent spot to see anyone approaching.'

Elizabeth breathed a sigh of relief, but neither was pleased when the growing light of dawn brought with it a light mist that thickened over the next hour.

Unfortunately, although the ground was predominately flat there were numerous hollows into which the fog settled to create seas of whiteness. The previously brightening sky dulled to give the terrain a monotone sheen and the coldness that had been kept at bay throughout the night seeped in through Lewis's clothes and made him shiver.

Elizabeth, who had been standing at the back of the barn looking in the opposite direction, joined Lewis and he didn't complain. By now the fog had coalesced to form a wall that cut them off from seeing the mound and even the main house, but one matter remained clear, and Lewis's grim expression conveyed that to Elizabeth:

'You reckon he'll come soon, don't you?' she said, her voice catching with fear that she tried to suppress. She grimaced when he nodded. 'How many men do you think he'll have with him?'

'He sent only one man after me, but he hired plenty more to lie in wait for us in Liberty. For his final act of revenge, he'll make sure we can't fight him off.'

Elizabeth provided a forlorn smile. 'Unless the fog clears, we won't even get to see how many come.'

'Then listen.'

Elizabeth opened her mouth to continue asking nervous questions but got Lewis's hint that she should quieten. Kneeling together behind the low barn wall they listened, looking into the blankness, waiting.

With nothing to see time passed slowly. There were no animal or bird sounds and only the gradual changes in the thickness of the fog that let them see more or less of the ground around the barn helped to alleviate the boredom.

The tedium had become so disheartening that it was with some surprise that a shape appeared. Lewis tensed, but then saw that it was just the corner of the house.

'The fog's lifting,' Elizabeth said, sounding relieved.

'Don't be. If Norton is going to attack, it'll be now.'

They waited. Lewis gazed at the dim smudge that was the main building, hoping to see more details on it as proof that the fog really was clearing, but it disappeared from view, extinguishing that hope.

Then he heard a noise, a moving of pebbles over pebbles, but the fog's sensory deprivation ensured he couldn't tell where it'd come from.

The noise came again. He strained his hearing, but he was unable to discern its direction. He looked to the other side of the barn, seeing only the wall.

Elizabeth tapped his shoulder and he swung round to look where she was pointing. A shape was emerging from the fog; the form was close to the ground and gradually discerned into that of a person crawling towards them.

Lewis trained his gun on the form, waiting until he was sure who it was, and then was glad he had showed restraint when the person raised a hand and he saw that it was Marshal Ingersoll.

Lewis waved and in response Ingersoll pointed to the side of the barn and raised four fingers. Lewis nodded then watched him crawl on towards the house, presumably to warn Harlan and Cameron.

Lewis turned to Elizabeth and pointed to the edge of the barn furthest away from the direction the hidden assailants were waiting.

Without comment Elizabeth paced that way while keeping her head down and took up a position in the opposite corner to the pile of rotting wood under which Mason Crockett's body lay. With her rifle aimed at the other end of the barn, she waited.

When Lewis was sure she was in the safest position, he crawled towards the other end of the barn where he adopted the same posture as Elizabeth had. He looked along the length of the wall, presuming someone would risk coming over before long.

All was quiet, the solid block of fog beyond the wall pressing in like a tangible force that seemed to suppress all sound. The fog was so thick even Elizabeth was visible only because he knew where she was, her form like a lump of rock in the corner of the barn, unmoving and quiet.

131

He heard a low gasp, perhaps of pain as someone stubbed their toe. A replying noise sounded: Lewis couldn't be sure what he had heard, but he imagined that another man had told the first, who had made a noise, to quieten.

Then they came.

A man paced up to the wall and looked into the barn with a hand to his brow.

Lewis had prepared himself to remain calm and although the sight made him flinch, he didn't move other than to align his gun and tighten his trigger finger a mite. The man beckoned backwards, but in making that movement he looked towards Lewis's corner of the barn.

They exchanged eye contact. Lewis fired, hitting the man in the side, a second rifle blast from Elizabeth sending him spinning away.

A shouted demand to get down sounded, followed by scurrying feet.

Accepting he wouldn't get another easy target Lewis bobbed up to look over the wall. He could see nothing other than the still body of the shot man. But hidden away in the fog, rapid footfalls sounded.

A shot tore out to his left and nearer to the house, then another, but he couldn't tell whether it was the attackers or his brothers who had fired.

In the other corner of the barn Elizabeth waved, asking what she should do, and with a downward gesture Lewis signified that she should stay where she was.

He took his own advice and hunkered back down in the corner. Being unable to see what was happening meant he was as likely to shoot one of his own brothers as hit any of the attackers.

Rapid gunfire erupted, this time from several directions, as people clearly locked horns. A man cried out. Lewis cocked his head to one side while he replayed the sound in his mind, deciding it hadn't sounded like anyone he knew.

Another burst of explosive gunfire tore out along with shouted orders. The words weren't discernible, but, hearing many different voices, Lewis reckoned there were more than just the handful of men Ingersoll had counted.

Lewis still forced himself to stay put, letting them come to him.

He heard someone ask a question and although he didn't pick up all the words it sounded as if that man was asking for directions. But more importantly Lewis clearly heard the last word: Norton.

That discovery changed Lewis's mind about his tactics. With a quick gesture to Elizabeth to tell her not to move he got to his feet and, hunched over, walked to the front of the barn towards the shooting.

'Watch out!' Elizabeth screeched.

From the corner of his eye Lewis saw her move, his quick reactions letting him judge the direction of the problem. He turned at the hip, sighting the man leaping over the back wall.

His first shot caught the man full in the stomach,

sending him reeling to land propped up against the wall.

He put a second slug in him, then turned and ran for the front wall. He vaulted it and hunkered down, listening for further comments and noises to emerge from the fog.

Long moments passed in which he heard nothing. Then, unheralded, three shapes emerged from the fog. Tendrils of mist wrapped around their legs, their forms indistinct.

With no clues as to who they were, Lewis waited. Slowly they became more distinct, but still Lewis couldn't see who these men were. Then he realized he was seeing the backs of a line of men and they were walking backwards towards him.

He stood, seeing a fourth and a fifth man appear. The endmost men looked to the centre, implying these were the extent of the forces aligned against them, but still they backed away, their focus being on the house.

Hunkered down in such a prominent position Lewis would stand no chance when they turned. He ran his gazes along them, hoping to see which one was Norton so he could be sure to get him, but their forms were too indistinct.

Pace by pace the line of men approached. The situation couldn't continue for much longer without somebody noticing him.

Sure enough, the man at the far end looked to his side again. He flinched, catching sight of Lewis from the corner of his eye. A cry of warning formed then died on his lips as Lewis dispatched him with a low shot to the back.

Then Lewis splayed gunfire at the next man. Elizabeth joined him by leaping up and firing, but at the same man.

Lewis turned and vaulted over the wall to duck down from their view, not waiting to see if the man had survived. He reloaded with rapid dexterity then launched himself to the side to ensure he was in a different position to the one they would expect. He rolled and scrambled along behind the wall until he was five yards closer to Elizabeth.

He moved to rise but had only enough time to plant a hand to the ground to lever himself up when Norton leapt over the wall before him, an arm strapped down to his side.

Lewis fired upwards at Norton's chest while Norton was still in the air. He was rewarded with a cry of pain before Norton tumbled down, but his body landed over Lewis's legs pinning him to the ground.

Lewis tried to push his still form off but, lying awkwardly, he failed to dislodge him at the first attempt, so he started to slip his legs out instead.

Two men appeared beyond the wall peering down at him with both their guns already aimed. Lewis jerked to the side, scrambling out from under his burden, and fired blind, but twin shots tore out.

Lewis fired again, then got to his knees, but it was to face the sight of the two men tumbling forwards over the wall. One man had been shot in the chest by Elizabeth, the other in the back by Cameron who appeared from behind the wall, his form becoming clearer as he approached. As Lewis now saw, the fog was lifting.

'Obliged,' Lewis said as he paced round to stand over Norton's body. 'How many more?'

'We got more than Marshal Ingersoll reckoned was out there already.'

'Harlan, Thomas, Ingersoll?'

'They're all fine,' Cameron said gesturing backwards at the men emerging behind him. 'We reckon we all got to plug at least one apiece.'

'I got two,' Harlan said, joining Cameron.

'That's one less than I got,' Ingersoll said, patting him on the arm.

Lewis relaxed slightly as the inevitable boasting began about each man's role in the fight.

'I got more than the rest of you put together,' he said, smiling for the first time since he'd arrived at his old home.

'I got none,' Thomas said.

Harlan slapped him on the back. 'But that's not the story you'll tell when we get home. You did as much as anyone did.'

'You sure did,' Cameron said. 'And it was good to have the Millers and Coltaines fighting on the same side for once.'

Thomas smiled. 'I'll be sure to tell my brothers that.'

'You do that,' Lewis said. 'But we still need to check that this is over.'

'Agreed,' Ingersoll said. 'I'll scout around now the fog's lifting. Nobody take anything for granted yet.'

'And we still have one final question to answer,' Lewis said. He looked at Thomas then pointed at the body at his feet. 'Is this the man you met in Redemption?'

Thomas moved over to take Lewis's place while Lewis backed away to put an arm around Elizabeth's shoulder. He gave her a brief hug while whispering words of encouragement.

'I just want this to be over,' she murmured.

As Lewis grunted that he agreed, Thomas knelt beside the body, then jerked back nodding.

Lewis couldn't help but clench a fist in triumph. He disentangled himself from holding Elizabeth then walked over towards the body.

'Are you sure?' he asked.

'It looks like Norton Crockett.' Thomas bent down and rolled the body over. It landed heavily but one look at the face was enough for him. 'Yeah. I only met him the once nine months ago, but that was enough. I—'

The body lurched, a gun swinging up in the assumed dead man's hand. A single shot tore into Thomas's chest sending him flying backwards.

Lewis had been starting to wish that Norton were still alive just so he could question him before he killed him. That thought fled from his mind as he fired into Norton's body. He kept on firing until he had no effect other than to make the body twitch.

Then he walked over the body of the man who had tried to destroy his family and hunkered down beside Thomas, as did Harlan and Cameron, but they could do nothing for him.

Thomas had been shot in the heart.

'Just when our families had become reconciled,' Cameron said, laying a hand on Thomas's still shoulder, 'this had to happen.'

'I never thought I'd be sad to see a Miller die,' Harlan murmured, 'but Thomas was a good man.'

'He was,' Lewis said. 'But what will the Millers think of this?'

CHAPTER 13

'Stay here,' Marshal Ingersoll said. 'I'll tell them the bad news.'

Cameron shook his head. 'No matter what the reaction, I have to be there.'

Ingersoll considered the three Coltaine brothers and although they hadn't discussed the matter on the journey back to White Ridge he received a nod from each.

'But just Cameron,' Lewis said. 'He's the calmest.'

Cameron acknowledged the compliment with a grim smile then filed in beside Ingersoll to head to the Millers' trading post.

They had visited the post first as they thought they owed Thomas that courtesy. But his unfortunate death had ensured that their journey from Fort Lord had been a sombre one despite the move towards he and Harlan becoming reconciled with Lewis.

With the journey due to take a week they had buried Thomas's body alongside his brother's in

Parker's Gulch. Although now that they'd arrived back at White Ridge, Cameron couldn't help but think that the lack of a body would further enflame the situation.

Ingersoll reached the door first then backhanded it open. He called inside, then again until a bleary-eyed Ward arrived in the main store area, stinking of whiskey as usual. When he saw Cameron he straightened up from his stooped posture.

'I'm not answering no questions when he's here,' he proclaimed.

'I'm not here to ask any,' Ingersoll said, using a grave tone to forewarn Ward of the bad news to come.

Ward narrowed his eyes, picking up on the hint, but he still glared at Cameron. When he reached the door and saw the others lined up thirty yards from the post, his anger grew.

'Then what in tarnation are they all here for?'

'It's about Thomas,' Cameron said.

Ward ran his gaze over the assembled people again, presumably checking that Thomas wasn't there, then called inside for Jacob to join him.

Everyone stayed quiet and nobody met anyone else's eye until he arrived. After Jacob had cast a surly glare at Cameron, Ward asked the question they'd all dreaded.

'Is Thomas dead, then?'

Ingersoll frowned. 'I'm sorry, but he is.'

'Guess that's what we expected when the Coltaines

rode off with you. Where's his body?'

'We had to bury him. The journey back was a—'

'Again! You wouldn't let us have Stacy's body for a year. Then you stole it. Now you're doing the same with Thomas.'

'It's not like that,' Cameron said, stepping forward.

Ward sneered. 'I'm not listening to you.'

Cameron kept his voice low and sombre. 'I know that, but we have a long story to tell. Even if you don't want to hear it now, know this, Thomas was a good man and he died at the hands of the same man who killed your Stacy. We all dealt with that man together.'

'What you saying?' Ward spluttered.

Cameron took a deep breath. 'I'm saying that Stacy didn't die twelve years ago. Jesse killed the wrong man and he returned that body to you. Stacy has been living in Parker's Gulch for the last twelve years, but three months ago he got killed when—'

'Enough!' Ward roared, slapping his hands over his ears. 'I don't want to hear no more tall tales from the Coltaines.'

'Yeah,' Jacob snapped. 'Get off our land.'

Cameron opened his mouth to relate a story that he'd have dismissed as too bizarre if someone had told it to him, but Ingersoll jerked his head towards their horses to signify they should back away.

'We'll leave now,' Ingersoll said, 'but I'll come back later and explain some more about what we found out.'

'I don't want to hear no more lies,' Ward whined.

'No lies,' Ingersoll said, backing away. 'Thomas is lying alongside your brother in Parker's Gulch and I'm really sorry he died.'

'We all are,' Cameron said.

With that comment Ingersoll and Cameron headed back to their horses. Cameron heard the Millers muttering to each other, dismissing their story as being too preposterous before the door slammed shut.

At a slow pace they rode away from the post, only speeding up when it was out of sight.

'Not go well?' Harlan asked, breaking the silence.

'Nope,' Cameron said, glancing at Ingersoll.

'I'll leave them to ponder for a day or so,' Ingersoll said, 'then try again. If I can't get through to them, I'll wait until they visit the saloon.'

Cameron frowned then looked at his brothers who both returned sour expressions that confirmed they thought it unlikely they'd listen to what he had to say.

Then Ingersoll veered away to head back to town leaving the brothers to complete a homecoming that would be more subdued than they'd have liked. Each man was tense as they waited to confirm that nothing untoward had happened while they'd been away.

The sight of Mary and Esther running outside and the huge cheery waves they both provided removed that worry. For a while they put aside their concerns.

Mary and Cameron embraced while Harlan hugged his family; Mary's smile grew even larger

142

when she saw that Lewis had returned with Elizabeth.

'Is he staying?' she asked.

'I don't know yet,' Cameron said, 'but wherever he goes, he'll always be welcome here.'

She breathed a sigh of relief. 'A family feud ended at last.'

'One of them has ended,' Cameron murmured.

'It needs a bit of work,' Cameron said.

Lewis considered the rotting pile of timbers nestling in a mounded heap of moss and mildew. This was the first home that their father had built until the brothers had built a larger home a hundred yards away.

'It sure does,' Lewis said, kicking a log and watching it disintegrate into powder.

'But you'll get plenty of help.'

'That eager to get me out of the house, eh?'

Lewis smiled and Cameron smiled in return. Two weeks ago that comment would have sparked an argument but not now.

'Maybe it'll help us all. Jesse was on his own, but you're not. If you stay, having somewhere to call your own might be for the best.'

Lewis sighed while thinking back to the home he'd built. It was a place that gave him too many bad memories and to which he didn't want to return. But maybe here. . . .

'I could stay, I guess.' He shrugged. 'But if I do, I doubt I'll ever get round to fully forgiving Jesse. You do know that, don't you?'

'And I doubt we'll ever get round to not liking him, but that's no reason why we can't get on.'

Lewis nodded. Although he still didn't like Jesse, he had become less annoyed since he'd discovered that they had both accidentally killed an innocent man.

'I'll think about staying, then.'

'You'll do more than think about it,' Cameron said in a stern tone, although he was smiling. 'Elizabeth is a good woman and after the terrible thing Norton Crockett did to you, she's the sort of person you need to be with.'

Lewis hadn't mentioned Elizabeth's tragic history and it would probably never feel appropriate to do so. He contented himself with a non-committed answer:

'It's more complex than that. We have plenty to discuss before we make any final decisions.' Lewis looked around, considering the land where he'd grown up. 'But if it's all right with you, we'll do that discussing here. If in a month it feels right to stay, then we'll get some paint and liven this place up.'

Cameron nodded with approval then pointed at a jointed length of gnawed wood lying on the ground that had once been a window.

'And make some new shutters for the window.'

'And make the corral larger.'

Cameron laughed loudly. The posts had fallen over long before the house had and the useless corral had once been a common family joke. He opened his mouth presumably to continue their joking, but then closed it and pointed over Lewis's shoulder.

Lewis turned to see that Harlan was running towards them from the main house. There was a slope to run up and while waving his arms to gather their attention, he was bounding along as fast as he could.

Lewis and Cameron stood in silence until he arrived then had to wait as Harlan gathered his breath.

'It's Elizabeth,' he spluttered finally. 'She's gone.'

Cameron shot Lewis a forlorn look.

'I'm sorry,' he murmured. 'But perhaps she's just gone to—'

'No!' Harlan said, now finding his voice. 'It's not that. It's the Millers. They've kidnapped her.'

When Lewis arrived back at the house, Mary blurted out the story of what had happened, and it wasn't a cheering one.

She and Elizabeth had set off for town so Mary could show her White Ridge and hopefully persuade her that the town was somewhere she'd want to settle down. They'd been midway to town when the Miller brothers had blocked their route and demanded that Elizabeth go with them.

Mary had been ready to ride on through, but Elizabeth had told her she'd be fine and had gone

145

with them meekly without a fight. But even if she'd been meek, the Coltaine brothers agreed they wouldn't react in the same way.

'I knew it'd come to this,' Harlan said. 'The surviving Millers know only one way to behave.'

Lewis said nothing, having already decided what he'd do, and so everyone looked at Cameron, presuming he'd be the voice of reason.

'They've taken a member of our family,' he said. 'This isn't a matter for Marshal Ingersoll. We'll deal with it.'

'Good,' Harlan said with a firm slap of a fist against thigh before he moved to leave, but Cameron shook his head.

'You'll stay here,' he said. 'We don't know what they're planning and we need to make sure everyone here is safe.'

'But,' Harlan murmured, 'I can't let you face them on your own.'

'Two Coltaines,' Lewis said, speaking for the first time since they'd returned, 'against two Millers. Those odds aren't good for them.'

With a quick series of curt nods to each other the matter was settled and Cameron and Lewis rode off leaving Harlan to protect the house and their families.

'Why do you reckon they took her, out of all of us?' Cameron asked when the post came into view.

'They had to make us pay somehow and this is the easiest way.' Lewis slapped his gun. 'But they'll get a heap more trouble than they ever expected.'

'Agreed.' Cameron pointed ahead. 'We'll ride up to the post and give them a chance to back down before we—'

'No risks,' Lewis muttered. 'We'll do this my way and give them no choice but give her up or die. You'll stay outside in case they run. I'll go in.'

Cameron considered Lewis's steely gaze then nodded.

Without further discussion they rode closer, taking a route that kept them out of view from the main window. Fifty yards from the post they dismounted then made their hurried way over to the building, running doubled over.

They stopped beside the corner post of a fence where Lewis bade Cameron stay put with a brief downward gesture. Then he ran for the door to stand beside it.

He listened at the door, hearing nothing. He mouthed to Cameron that it was quiet then mentally rehearsed the actions needed to get in quickly.

Then he kicked open the door and launched himself through the doorway, keeping low. He dived to the floor to confuse the people inside, rolling over a shoulder to land on his knees where he sighted the people by the counter.

He swung his gun round to aim at them then stilled when he saw that Ward was holding Elizabeth from behind. The shock on Ward's face showed that he'd surprised them.

'Let her go,' Lewis muttered.

'Can't do that,' Ward said. Then he moved her to the side so that Lewis could see the gun he'd pressed against her back.

To Ward's side Jacob stood up from behind the counter. He held a rifle on Lewis.

'Harm her,' Lewis said, 'and neither of you will walk out of here alive.'

This comment made Jacob gulp, but Ward merely sneered.

'No matter what you do, she'll die first and that means we'll have got what we wanted. Now drop your gun or I'll kill her.'

Lewis weighed up the situation, biding his time for as long as he dared in the hope that something would happen that'd give him a distraction, but neither brother moved. And Elizabeth's apparent composure was snapping as she started to shake.

He raised his left hand and nodded.

'All right,' he said, then opened his hand so that his gun swung loose on a finger.

'Drop the gun and kick it over here,' Ward demanded.

Lewis did as ordered although he kicked the gun using minimal force so it stopped a few feet from Ward and Elizabeth, giving him a chance to reach it if the opportunity presented itself.

'What now?' he asked.

'Now,' Ward said, glaring over Lewis's shoulder, 'you'll tell your brother to come out into the open.'

Lewis glanced through the window. He saw nothing, but presumably Ward had caught sight of him getting closer to the house.

'Cameron,' Lewis shouted, 'they've seen you. Stand up, drop your gun, then walk away.'

He looked at Ward, who provided a nod of approval. Then they waited.

Lewis presumed that despite his orders Cameron would work out that the assault had not gone well and he would have a plan of his own to retaliate. But when Cameron came into view through the window, he appeared to do everything Lewis had asked. He discarded his gun, making his action obvious, then turned on his heel and slowly walked away.

'Is he the only one?' Ward asked.

'Yeah,' Lewis said. 'Just the two of us came.'

Ward nodded then edged to the side to look through the window.

'Hey,' he shouted, 'move quicker.'

Cameron kept moving at the same slow pace and so in irritation Jacob swung his rifle round to the window. He aimed without care, but even so when he fired the slug whined into the ground close to Cameron's receding feet.

To his credit Cameron didn't speed up and with mounting annoyance Ward joined Jacob in swinging his gun up to aim through the window.

This was the kind of distraction Lewis had hoped he'd get.

He jerked forward aiming to throw himself at

Ward, but Elizabeth had already had the same idea. She tore her arm away from Ward's grip then elbowed him in the stomach making him fold.

Lewis stopped himself then leapt at Jacob instead. He grabbed his right arm and thrust it up high.

Jacob held on to the rifle as the two men battled for supremacy. They rocked back and forth, each man trying to take control of the rifle, but with Jacob's tight grip and sounds of a scuffle coming from behind, Lewis released his hold of the weapon.

He bunched both hands together and delivered a two-handed backswipe that cracked Jacob's head back and knocked him into the counter. With Jacob's chest exposed Lewis thundered a short-arm jab into his guts that made him gasp in pain.

Bent double, Jacob staggered forwards and then it was a simple matter of Lewis grabbing his shoulders, swinging him round, and running him at the counter. His head collided with the rim with a dull thud, making him collapse.

Then Lewis turned on his heel to see that Elizabeth had wrested the gun from Ward and Ward had stepped back to consider her, his eyes wide open with fear.

'Good work, Elizabeth,' Lewis said.

'You shouldn't have worried about me,' Elizabeth said, her voice high pitched and full of emotion.

'Of course I should.'

Elizabeth nodded then looked away from Ward to stare at him.

'Are you trying to tell me that you really do care about me?'

Lewis considered the comatose Jacob at his feet and the cowering Ward.

'This flea-bitten post wouldn't have been my first choice for a place to admit it, but yes, I care for you. Finding out that these two varmints had kidnapped you and the thought of what they might do was too much to bear. I couldn't live through that again.'

She breathed a hoarse sigh of relief.

'But,' she whispered, speaking slowly, 'they didn't kidnap me.'

Her comment made Ward relax and grin.

'What do you mean?' Lewis murmured.

'I mean that when I stayed here before, I planned all this. I wanted you to think they'd kidnapped me.'

Lewis swayed with the shock. 'Just to find out if I cared?'

'Yup.'

'There were better ways of doing that.'

'There weren't. I had to know that it mattered to you that I'd gone. I had to know that you were suffering the pain of losing someone before I told you the truth.'

'What truth?'

'That in all the time we've known each other and despite all the times we've talked about your quest for vengeance, you've never once wanted to talk about my quest.' She swung the gun round to aim it at Lewis. 'But you will now.'

'We did talk,' Lewis murmured, an inkling of what she meant hitting him. 'You wanted me to find the man who killed your husband.'

'I did, and yet you never asked that man's name.' She waited for Lewis to reply, but he said nothing, not wanting to hear the rest. 'But let's see if you can work it out. He took a job from a man who had someone on his tail. He became a decoy to buy that man a few hours' leeway and he died for the sake of a cheap horse.'

'Raymond Templeton?' Lewis murmured.

'Sure. And after you gunned him down, his brother wasted the last months of his life chasing you, but I had the better idea to make you suffer.'

Lewis sighed. 'At the end Maxwell had the same idea, but I told him: killing Raymond Templeton wasn't my fault. It was an accident.'

'So you claimed, but that's what happens when you seek vengeance. People die and you make new enemies.'

'I know, but you didn't act like I was your enemy.' Lewis considered her stern expression and steady gun. 'Surely everything you said to me and everything we did couldn't have been a lie.'

'It wasn't,' she said, her voice cracking for the first time. 'At first I feigned feelings for you, but then real feelings took over. I realized that just as you'd repeated Jesse's mistake, I was repeating Norton's mistake. So I tried to persuade you to give up. I decided that if you didn't go after Norton Crockett,

I'd move on too, but you wouldn't. So I have to see it through.'

Lewis spread his hands. 'You're right, so see it through. I won't stop you.'

CHAPTER 14

While he walked away Cameron picked out a route back to the post that would keep him out of the view of anyone looking at him. When he reached a hollow he risked looking back. The post was no longer visible.

Cameron reckoned that meant he'd completed his side of the deal.

With his head down he hurried along the length of the hollow until he reached a point where he was side on to the post and had a view that didn't contain windows. Then he hurried to the building.

He consoled himself with the observation that since receiving his ultimatum he'd heard no gunfire so he wasn't too late to help yet. When he reached the wall, he stood and caught his breath then scurried beneath the window to reach the door. There, he stood and listened but he heard nothing.

He backhanded the door open then edged inside.

By the counter Elizabeth was standing beside Ward while Lewis had his back to him. He couldn't see Jacob but the three people were all looking at each other, a confrontation clearly in progress.

Then Cameron registered that the only armed person was Elizabeth and she appeared to be holding her gun on Lewis.

She noticed him and flinched. Slowly she lowered the gun, her action making Lewis sag his shoulders.

'What's happening here?' Cameron demanded.

For several seconds nobody replied until Lewis swung round to face him.

'Nothing,' he said. 'We've sorted everything out.'

'But didn't she have a gun?'

'It was mighty tense for a while. But it's all fine now.' Lewis turned to Elizabeth and she gave a brief nod.

Still bemused by what he thought he'd seen Cameron shuffled towards them. When he joined Lewis, Jacob stood up from beside the counter, rubbing his head.

Jacob coughed and glanced at Ward, then coughed again before he spoke.

'Perhaps we didn't fully understand the situation,' he said. 'We gather it wasn't your fault that Thomas died.'

'No,' Cameron said cautiously, 'it wasn't.'

'And we're pleased you found out that Stacy got to live a full life when we thought him dead.'

Cameron nodded, lost for the right words to say,

but Lewis spoke up.

'And the rest,' he urged.

Jacob licked his lips while Ward shuffled from foot to foot. Then he took a deep breath.

'This is over,' Ward said. 'There's no need to carry on our family feud.'

'That sure is a relief,' Cameron murmured.

'We won't be seeking you out to talk or buying you drinks in the saloon, but we won't avoid the Coltaines no more.'

Cameron favoured Jacob and Ward with a smile for probably the first ever time.

'And that's all we could ever ask for,' he said.

A celebration was going on inside the house.

Happy chatter and even bursts of singing drifted up into the evening air, but Lewis and Elizabeth stayed outside, as they had done since the others had gone inside an hour ago.

Since leaving the Millers' trading post that afternoon they'd yet to speak and even after being left alone, they'd not discussed the incident.

Lewis was starting to wonder whether he should be the one to mention the subject when she turned to him and he could see in her troubled eyes that she'd had the same thought.

'I'm sorry for what happened today,' she said simply.

'I'm sorry for what happened four months ago,' he said.

They sat in companionable silence for a while until the growing cold made her shiver. Lewis removed his jacket and wrapped it around her shoulders.

'I know that now.' She sighed. 'And I guess I've known it was an accident for a while. Despite what you did, I've grown to care for you, but once I'd set myself on the path of getting vengeance, I couldn't stop.'

'I know. That's why I didn't stop you.'

'But you did,' she said, smiling, 'in your own way.'

Her statement and warm smile cheered him.

Then, with the uncomfortable subject broached and the seeds of a potential resolution opened up, they linked arms and together they headed inside to rejoin the rest of the Coltaine family.